DATE DUE		

FIC
GIF

31280111051921
Giff, Patricia
Reilly.

Water Street

water
street

Also by
PATRICIA REILLY GIFF

FOR MIDDLE-GRADE READERS

FOR YOUNGER READERS

water
street

PATRICIA REILLY GIFF

WENDY
LAMB
BOOKS

Published by Wendy Lamb Books
an imprint of Random House Children's Books
a division of Random House, Inc.
New York

WENDY LAMB BOOKS and colophon are
trademarks of Random House, Inc.

www.randomhouse.com/kids

Educators and librarians, for a variety of teaching tools,
visit us at www.randomhouse.com/teachers

Library of Congress Cataloging-in-Publication Data
Giff, Patricia Reilly.
Water Street / Patricia Reilly Giff.
p. cm.
Summary: In the shadow of the construction of the Brooklyn Bridge,
eighth-graders and new neighbors Bird Mallon and Thomas Neary make
some decisions about what they want to do with their lives.
ISBN-13: 978-0-385-73068-6 (trade)—ISBN-13: 978-0-385-90097-3 (glb)
ISBN-10: 0-385-73068-3 (trade)—ISBN-10: 0-385-90097-X (glb)
[1. Self-realization—Fiction. 2. Family—Fiction. 3. Irish Americans—
Fiction. 4. Brooklyn Bridge (New York, N.Y.)—History—Fiction.
5. Brooklyn (New York, N.Y.)—History—19th century—Fiction.] I. Title.
PZ7.G3626Wav 2006
[Fic]—dc22
2006002024

Printed in the United States of America
The text of this book is set in 12-point Goudy.
Book design by Kenny Holcomb

10 9 8 7 6 5 4 3 2

First Edition

With love
to
James Patrick Giff,
Immortality

I am so grateful to Wendy Lamb for her unfailing support and belief in my books;

to George Nicholson, my agent, for all the years of advice and friendship;

to Kathy Winsor Bohlman for her expertise in more areas than I can count;

to my three children: Jim, who shares the world of books and ideas with me; Alice, who reads and warms my heart with her praise; and Bill, who has spent so many hours on my manuscripts, thoughtfully reviewing, and adding immeasurably to my work. I am blessed by their love.

And always, gratitude to my husband, Jim, who makes life as sweet as it is.

Summer 1875

BEFORE

Thomas had made himself a notebook with cardboard covers and sewed in the pages, but if the book wasn't handy, he used anything, paper bags from the market, or even the edges of the newspaper.

He wrote stories about anything he saw, and he saw a lot. He walked through the streets of Brooklyn along the water, or leaned against the store windows on Livingston Street watching people hurrying along, making up stories about this one or that one.

Sometimes he thought about how it had started, this writing of his, and his mind jumped to the woman's collar and the cuff of her sleeve with a wrist barely visible.

Strange, he couldn't picture her face, and he didn't know her name anymore, but he knew what she'd been doing, teaching him letters, teaching him words, leaning forward, and he remembered something she had said: "With just the sweep of a pen, Thomas, you can change the world, all of it."

He hadn't known what she was talking about then; he'd thought it was impossible. But he'd known it for a long time now, ever since he'd begun to write, really write. He could decide whatever world he wanted on paper, and that was the world it would be.

But now he turned the corner to see the bridge towers that were going up; someday there'd be a span crossing the East River, reaching from one tower to the other. In front was Water Street.

Grand name for a street.

Halfway down was a brownstone building with a sign: TOP FLOOR VACANT. You could probably see the towers from up there. You could look down and see everything. There must be dozens of stories right in that street.

Pop was ready to move again, Thomas could see that. They'd lived in four, no, five different places in the past few years. Thomas hurried back along the way he'd come. If Pop was around, he'd tell him about the place. And even if he didn't come in until the middle of the night, Thomas would wait up for him.

Water Street.

CHAPTER ONE
{BIRD}

Bird clattered down the stairs in back of Mama, past Mrs. Daley's on the first floor, and Sullivan the baker at the window in front. Outside she and Mama held hands, swinging them back and forth as they hurried along Water Street.

"Hot." Bird squinted up at the sun that beat down, huge and orange.

"Even this early," Mama agreed.

For a quick moment, they stopped to look at the tower standing by itself at the edge of the East River. One day it would be part of a great bridge.

What would it be like to stand on top, arms out, seeing the world the way a bird would? she wondered.

Bird, her nickname.

She pulled her heavy hair off her neck. "Mrs. Daley says they'll never be able to finish that bridge. She says it will collapse under its own weight and tumble right into the river."

They said it together, laughing: "Mrs. Daley says more than her prayers."

"Still," Bird said, "half of Brooklyn says the same thing."

"Not I," Mama said, "and not your da. We know anything is possible, otherwise we'd still be in the Old Country scrabbling for a bit of food."

Bird glanced at Mama, the freckles on her nose, her hair with a few strands of gray coming out of her bun ten minutes after she'd looped it up: Mama's strong face, which Da always said was just like Bird's. She couldn't see that. When she looked in the mirror, she saw the freckles, the gray eyes, and the straight nose, but altogether it didn't add up to Mama's face.

She was glad to reach the house on the corner, the number 112 painted over the door, and the vestibule out of the sun.

They climbed the stairs, the light dim as they stopped to catch their breath on each landing. "Let me." Bird took the blue cloth medicine bag that hung over Mama's shoulder. "It seems your patients are always on the top floor."

"Ah, isn't it so," Mama said, holding her side. "And the babies always coming in the dead cold of winter, or on steamy days like this."

Bird could feel the tick of excitement. Mama's words to her were deep inside her head: *"Only days until your thirteenth birthday. You're old enough to come with me for a birthing."* Bird's feet tapped it out on the steps: *a baby, a baby.*

She'd been helping Mama for a long time, chopping her healing herbs and drying them, helping to wash old Mrs. Cunningham, bringing tonic to Mr. Harris. But this! A baby coming! She couldn't have been more excited.

On the fifth floor, the door was half-open. Two children played under a window; an old man rocked in the one chair, a toddler on his lap pulling at his beard. "The daughter's inside," he said.

In the bedroom, the daughter lay in a nest of blankets, her head turned away, her hair in long dark strands over the covers. She made a deep sound in her throat, then turned toward them, and Bird could see how glad she was that Mama was there.

Who wouldn't be glad to see Mama, who knew all about healing, about birthing? Mama, who always made things turn out right.

Mama patted the woman's arm. "I know, Mrs. Taylor." She nodded at Bird. "Now here's what you'll do. You'll sit on the other side of the bed there. Hold her hand, and cool her forehead with a damp cloth."

Easy enough, Bird thought.

"And I'll have the work of it," the woman said before another pain caught her, blanching the color from her cheeks.

"You've done it all before." Mama leaned over to open her bag. "After three girls, there's nothing to the fourth, is there now?"

Mama made a tent of the blankets so she could help with the birth, and Bird went into the other room to fill a pan with water and wring out a rag. She stepped over the children as she went, bending down to touch the tops of their heads.

Back in the bedroom she ran the rag over the woman's neck and face. She held her hand during the pains for as long as she could stand it, then pulled her own hand away in between each one. Bird's hands were larger than Mama's already, but still she felt as if her fingers were being crushed in the woman's grip.

At first the woman talked a little, telling them that her husband wanted a boy, that he wouldn't forgive her if it was another girl, but after a while it was only her breathing Bird heard in that stifling room, and sometimes that sound in her throat, but Mama's voice was sure and soft, telling her it wouldn't be long.

Bird sat there thinking about the miracle of it, to be like Mama, to be able to do this. She wanted nothing more than that, to go up and down the streets of Brooklyn, with all that Mama knew in her head, the herbs to cure in a bag looped over her arm, the babies to birth. Bird watched Mama wipe her own forehead with her sleeve, then put her hands on the woman, pressing down and murmuring, "Take another breath, and as you let it out, push with me, push."

It went on and on, and the room was filled with that July heat, with air that never moved. Such a long day, and the sounds the woman made were much louder now, so loud that the two children came to the door, staring in, until Mama realized they were there. She reached with her foot to push the door and gently closed them out.

And then the smell of blood was in the room, and the

baby slid into Mama's hands, wet and glistening. "A girl." She handed her to Bird.

Too bad about the foolish husband, Bird thought, looking down at the baby, who was pale, and tiny, and crying weakly. "Beautiful," she breathed, then washed her with water from the pan and wrapped her in the receiving blanket Mama took from her bag.

Bird could feel the wetness in her eyes from the wonder of it, and the woman sighed and asked, "What's your name?"

"Bridget Mallon." The name sounded strange; no one called her anything but Bird.

"Bridget," the woman said. "Then that will be her middle name. Mary Bridget."

Bird felt a rush of tears. "For me? How can I ever—" She rocked the baby gently. This was just the beginning, her first baby, and there'd never be another like her. It was almost as if that baby were looking straight at her, and that she knew it, too. Mary Bridget. A person with a name.

Mama went into the other room to wash her hands, then came back to clean the woman.

Bird hated to give the baby up, but Mama raised her eyebrows, so she kissed the baby's cheek and put her into the woman's arms.

"How disappointed he'll be," the woman said.

"He's lucky," Bird said fiercely, then rinsed the woman's face one last time.

As they left the apartment, the old man pressed a few coins into Mama's hand. Bird knew at least one of those coins would make its way into the saving-for-the-farm box in the kitchen drawer. That box had been filling slowly for all the years she could remember.

She felt as if she hardly touched each step as she went down the stairs. At the landing she reached out to Mama. She didn't have a way with words, and it was hard to say what she felt, but Mama knew.

"I remember my first." She put her hands on Bird's shoulders. "You are like me, Birdie. You'll be a healer like I am. Better." She touched Bird's face. "I couldn't ask for more."

Could it be? Bird wondered. Would she ever know enough?

As they came outside, the church bells were chiming. Six o'clock, the day almost over!

And then she saw a horse and cart in front of their house; it was laden with boxes, and rickety furniture, and chair legs up in the air.

"Finally new tenants for the apartment upstairs," Bird said. "I hope there's a girl."

"Like himself, that husband, but he wanted a boy," Mama said, and they both smiled. Hands locked, they went up the flight of stairs. Bird's older sister, Annie, would be home from the box factory and sure to have a pot of coffee on the back of the stove for them, and a soda bread coming out of the oven. Maybe Hughie would be home, too, bent over the table reading his newspaper.

Bird wished for a glimpse of the new tenants, but they were nowhere in sight, and the door of the empty apartment upstairs was closed.

"Soon enough," Mama said, reading her mind again.

Nothing was ever soon enough for her. But then she remembered Mama's words: *"I couldn't ask for more."*

She said them over in her mind, words she'd never forget.

If only she could have held on to that day, held on to that moment forever, grasped it in her fists so it wouldn't escape.

If only.

CHAPTER TWO
{THOMAS}

Thomas thought about telling Pop it wasn't a good idea to leave the horse and cart out on the street like that. Anyone could take their stuff. And what about bringing the cart back to the livery stable over on Hudson Street? Hadn't Sweeney said he wanted them there before dark?

But Pop had one thing on his mind, and that was to find the nearest pub. He was too thirsty to listen to anything else.

Thomas took the bucket, still sloshing with water, from under the seat and held it up. The horse was as thirsty as Pop and gulped it all down, showing a thick pink tongue.

The baker on the first floor was moving back and forth in his shop as his assistant scurried around with trays of bread. It reminded Thomas that he hadn't eaten since breakfast.

He followed Pop down Water Street then, across Fulton,

past two or three pubs, until Pop finally stopped. "This one, I think." Pop squeezed his arm. "It looks like the pub in Granard, doesn't it?"

He'd forgotten again. Thomas had never been in Granard, where Pop had been born, never been in Ireland.

"Yes." Pop nodded. "A good place to quench that thirst of mine."

Thomas looked up: gold letters splashed across the window, GALLAGHER'S BAR AND GRILL, a green door and a pair of gaslights in front. It was larger than the one around the corner from the apartment they'd had in Greenpoint, and a lot like Carmody's, two blocks down from their last place in Flatbush. It was certainly large enough for dog fights or bare-knuckle boxing in the back room.

Pop looked at him uneasily. "I won't be long, Thomas."

"It's all right." Thomas waved his notebook, but before he could say anything else, Pop had pulled open the door and was standing at the bar.

Thomas watched him for a few minutes. Pop was good-looking, muscular, and his hair was almost gold even though it was getting a little thin on top. Thomas must have taken after his mother, whoever she was.

He walked toward the back through an alley that was narrow enough for him to touch the buildings on each side. It opened onto a small garden.

A surprise. Even though it was weedy, and a few smashed bottles were mixed in with the bushes, it had color: bunches of stalky yellow shoots, a rosebush, and a tree that spread its branches all the way to the fence.

He sank down to lean against the trunk of the tree, and

listened to the piano playing inside. The music sounded like "Murphy's Little Back Room," but all the player piano songs seemed alike to him.

He opened his book to a new page and wrote about the garden, leaving out the weeds and the broken bottles with their sharp necks.

He added a stone wall he had seen somewhere over in Manhattan once, and the window on Gallagher's back wall became the window of a house. He squinted as he wrote. He added paper shades that were pulled halfway up, so you could see inside.

All the house needed were people.

He could feel that in his chest. A family.

He'd seen a mother and a daughter at the end of the street before, holding hands as they walked. They looked alike, lots of curly hair, even though the mother's was caught up in back of her head. They looked as if they were glad to be together, as if they were on their way home to a cold ham dinner or maybe slices of leftover roast. Home to a family.

He wouldn't let the pencil move anymore. He had gotten too close to where he didn't want to be.

And then in spite of himself he began again, turning the page. He wrote about remembering how it felt to walk on the bare floor in the middle of the night. Where was Pop? His winter underwear wasn't enough in that freezing apartment. He wrote about going into the kitchen and leaning his head against the back door, hoping the woman with the lacy sleeves would come. He turned the page to write about sinking down on the floor, too afraid to call, and falling asleep when he saw the light coming in the window.

But that was a real world, and he didn't have to put it down on paper. He ripped the page out of the book, tore it into shreds, and threw them behind the tree, where they settled into the weeds.

It was getting dark now, dark enough to see the fireflies flitting around in that garden, and the piano was still for a moment.

He stood up to look in Gallagher's window, and saw men in the room behind the bar. They stood around two boys, maybe sixteen or seventeen, who had climbed into a make-shift ring.

He leaned on the sill; it didn't look like any of the matches he'd seen where the boxers wore long tight pants and shirts and tied their scarves on the ropes, boxers who shook hands before they danced around each other, jabbing their fists into the air.

These two were angry, enraged at each other. The one closest to him had dark hair that flopped over his forehead, and he glanced toward the window as he shrugged out of his jacket and let it fall to the floor in back of him.

The boy looked at Thomas just one second too long. The other boy, bigger, stronger, threw himself on top of the first boy, and they crashed together onto the floor, rolling over into one of the men in the corner.

Someone else kicked out at them, and then they were up, and instead of just the two fighting, half the men in the room were at it.

Thomas watched the one with the dark hair; he was graceful and strong. If he hadn't been so angry, he might have placed his punches better.

Now chairs were thrown, and someone's face was cut. Thomas looked for Pop, but he didn't see him, and the door of the back room was closed, so he couldn't see the bar in front. He hoped Pop was still sitting there on one of the stools, out of it.

He ran through the alley, scraping his arm on the cement wall, and out in front to see Pop coming down the two steps under the gaslights, holding on to the railing.

He went toward Pop, heart pounding, relieved that he hadn't been hurt in that fight. Pop put his hand on his shoulder. "I'm sorry I took so long, Thomasy. It's just the heat; I had to have something to cool me off."

He didn't look cool; in the flickering light his face was red and beads of sweat were on his forehead.

They walked back along Fulton to Water Street, the smell of the butcher shop strong as they passed, with its slabs of beef in the window, and sheep's heads with dull eyes that seemed to stare after them.

Thomas kept thinking about the boy with the dark hair, and his face when he went down. Had he been hurt?

They could see the tower that was rising on the Manhattan side of the East River. He wondered what it would be like to walk around eight or ten stories above the ground.

Pop's hand was still on his shoulder, a wide hand, long fingers. "Listen, Thomas. Maybe everything will be different this time."

He said that every time they moved, but Thomas nodded

as if he believed him. He wanted it to be true, wanted it so much, and he wanted to reach up and hug Pop, because his eyes looked so sad.

"A new start," Pop said as they stopped at the corner and waited to cross over to where the horse and cart waited for them. "A new apartment, Thomas. A new life."

A new world to write about.

CHAPTER THREE
{BIRD}

Mama's healing plants marched across the windowsill, waiting for a drink. Bird had promised her brother, Hughie, she'd water them this morning, and had forgotten all about it in her excitement over the baby. Next to Mama he was the most interested in the plants, not the way she and Mama were, for how they could heal, but for the look of them, the size of them, even for the feel of the damp earth they grew in.

One of her first memories: Hughie holding her up to touch a pink bud. "New like you, Birdie," he'd said.

She filled a jelly jar with water and dribbled it into the pots: more for the primroses, thirsty things, and a little less for the chives. She ran her finger over pots of soft moss, and in her head: *Moss to stop bleeding*. She tapped the top of a spiky plant: *Aloe for burns*.

She was writing all of it down in a book Mama had

made for her, but she knew most of it by heart now anyway.

Outside the window in front of her was Water Street. People sat on the stoops to escape the heat, and a line of dray horses clopped by.

The new tenants' cart was still there in front, the horse's head drooping; he was almost asleep. It was close to nine o'clock. What was the matter with those people anyway?

She angled her head to see better.

Her older sister, Annie, turned from the counter, looking almost like Hughie with her thick dark hair and sky-blue eyes. She wasn't good-looking like Hughie, though. She called herself plain, and Bird knew that was true. Annie hated the small scar like a dent in her cheek from where she had fallen once, but Bird loved Annie's face.

"You're watering the floor, Bird," Annie said.

"Watch out. I may water your feet and I think they're big enough as it is."

That made Annie laugh. "Any minute the plants are going to go, and you with them." She tapped her finger gently on the yeast dough she had rising in the yellow bowl. "Almost ready to bake."

She came over to stand next to Bird at the window, her hair tickling Bird's cheek.

"I think you're hoping the new tenant will be handsome and single," Bird said. "A beau for you."

"Not a bit of it." Annie gave her arm a tiny pinch.

At the table, Da looked up smiling. "At least let's hope it isn't someone who dances all night, rattling the floorboards over our heads."

Bird looked back at him, running his hand through that gray hair of his. He was broomstraw thin, tall, and a little bent, and she knew he didn't really care about how much noise the new tenants would make. Mama said he slept like a log.

Mama called him Sean Red, and once Bird had asked her why. Mama had wiped her hands on her apron. "His hair is the color of the carrots in the soup Annie makes," she had said, and they'd all laughed. Mama had glanced up at Da then, her hand to her mouth. "You've gone white, Sean. I never noticed."

Annie leaned forward. "Is that someone on the other side of the cart now?"

Yes, Bird saw two pairs of feet. She looked harder. Men's feet. "I think I'm going to get some air," she said.

"Is there anyone nosier in this world than Bird Mallon?" Annie had a glint in her eye.

"No one unless it's you," Bird said.

"Nothing wrong with a little curiosity," Da said.

"It's dark out," Mama said.

"Not that dark," Bird told her. "And I'm just going to walk up and down the block." She took a breath. "It's roasting in here." She pecked Da on the cheek, and went around the table to run her hand over Ma's shoulder.

She rushed down the stairs, passing Mrs. Daley's apartment on the first floor, then Sullivan's Bakery on the ground floor, closed for the night, with its baker cooking somewhere in back.

She slowed her steps as she reached the stoop outside, glad there were people all over the place. The new tenants would never think she was coming after them.

And there they were. She was close enough now to see those sticklike chairs piled up on the wagon, a couch with stuffing coming out of one arm, a mattress, and stacks of boxes. She swept her eyes toward the sky, as if she were looking at the stars, then glanced down to the street again: a boy and his father.

The father was under the weather; he must have been drinking for hours. He was singing "Sweet Rosie," or "Sweet Kate," or "Sweet Mary," stumbling over the back wheel, and "Sweet Kate" became "Jesus, Mary, and Joseph" under his breath.

She ducked her head the way Father Kinsella had told them to do when they heard the Holy Name.

The boy stood next to the wagon, skinny as a rail with sandy hair and baggy pants. He looked as if you'd raise dust if you took the rug beater to him.

A bitter disappointment.

He grinned when he saw her, almost as if he knew who she was. "What's your name?"

What nerve. "Bird," she said reluctantly.

"I thought it was something terrible, like Eldrida, from the look on your face." He tilted his head. "Prunes or lemons, maybe persimmons."

She could only imagine what a persimmon was. She grinned, trying to hide it from him as she looked up, catching a glimpse of Annie's face at the window. No beau for her. The boy was too young, the father too old.

And the boy was right in back of her, his neck thin as a pencil. "My name is Thomas," he said. "Thomas Neary."

She didn't answer.

"The horse's name is Alfred, in case you want to know." He screwed up his face. "Or maybe Fernando."

She had to laugh, and so did he. But Mr. Neary was outside hollering to two boys on the corner to give a hand. Bird and the new boy went back to help, one on each end of the mattress, dragging it up the stairs.

"Filthy stairs," someone said.

"Not so bad," she said with some guilt. After all, Mrs. Daley paid her to sweep them down every Saturday.

When they were finished moving everything upstairs, the brown couch in between the windows, a long table with feet like lions in the middle of the room, and the chairs all around, Mr. Neary wandered back and forth between the rooms. He fingered the velvet curtains, left by an earlier tenant, worn to the backing, but still a gorgeous purple color.

She and Thomas sat one on each end of the couch in the living room without much to say to begin with. She ran her hands over her skirt. She knew it was getting late and that she should go, but still—

She peeked at the things he had lined up on the table: a gray feather, a penknife with a white bone handle, and a book he had made himself, almost like her cure book. And real books with leather covers. Ten of them, maybe a dozen. How lucky he was.

At last she began. "Nice view of the new bridge going up from here," she said. "My father works there. My sister loves to cook, to bake really, and my mother is a healer. Half of Brooklyn knows her." What else? "My brother, Hughie—" She bit her lip. She didn't want to talk about Hughie. And why had she blurted all that out anyway? She reminded herself of their kitchen faucet. They'd turn it on and nothing happened. Then when they'd almost given up, water splashed out and out and they had a hard time stopping it.

But Thomas was hardly listening. He took a quick look over his shoulder and she thought he might be embarrassed about his father, who was out of sight, singing "Murphy's Little Back Room."

He stood up and wandered into the bedroom after his father. Without thinking, she pulled his homemade book an inch closer: pages filled with handwriting, but she didn't have time to read them.

There was a picture of a woman, though, torn out from a magazine. *A beauty called Lillie,* it said. She wore a hat with a plume and a silk gown; pearls the size of marbles were looped around her long neck, and her hands were clasped in front of her.

She really was a beauty.

There was writing scribbled on the bottom. She thought it said *Mother.*

He had a mother who looked like that?

But then a door slammed, and Mr. Neary's voice was cut off. Before she could even close the book, Thomas was back in the living room.

She felt her face redden as she pushed the book away, hoping he hadn't seen her looking at his things.

But he pointed to the window. "Stars out there. You're supposed to wish on them."

"What would you wish?" she asked.

He raised one shoulder, but she could see from the look on his face there was something he wanted.

"I want to be a healer," she said, "like my mother." She couldn't wait for it to begin. One more year of school, one long year left before she could go with Mama all the time.

She thought of the little baby. *Mary Bridget.*

All her days would be like the day she'd had today.

But Annie was calling from the stairs now. "Bird? Where did you get yourself? It's almost eleven o'clock."

She put her hand up to her mouth. Eleven, that late. "My sister," she said. "Five years older. She thinks she's my mother." She slid off the couch and waved at him over her shoulder on her way out the door.

CHAPTER FOUR
{THOMAS}

"So, Thomasy," Pop said, "a girl downstairs."

He tried not to grin. "Yes."

"Same age as you are? Lives right in the apartment below?"

"Yes." *A girl who swings hands with her mother. Eldrida.*

"You might want to clean yourself up a little then. Wash your face once in a while."

He didn't answer that. He wasn't sure the girl would care about it; he didn't care about it.

There were two bedrooms in the apartment, curtains blocking them off instead of doors. The larger one had a window, the other was smaller and without a window, boiling in summer, but cozy in the winter, and the last tenant had left a picture hanging there where the window might have been.

It showed a lighthouse standing on a jumble of gray rocks

with foamy white waves crashing up on them. But what he really liked about it was the square window three-quarters of the way up the lighthouse, lighted with a splash of yellow paint.

What would it be like to live there in back of that window with the warm candlelight? The waves looked stormy, dangerous, and you'd be up there with the rest of the family, looking down at it all with a fire going in the hearth and a hot stew on the stove.

He stood there running his hand over the frame. He'd leave the big room for Pop and take the one with the lighthouse.

"Have to bring the horse and wagon back to the livery place now," Pop said.

"I'll go with you." He could see Pop wasn't that steady on his feet.

Pop waved his hand. "It's been a long day. Stay here then, Thomas, get some sleep for yourself."

Thomas knew he'd bring the horse to the stable, then take himself back to Gallagher's.

"Listen, Pop," he said, "don't do that."

Pop raised his eyebrows. "Have to bring the horse back. We're late as it is. Sweeney is going to carry on about the extra hours; he's going to want more money. But too bad for Sweeney. You can't get blood out of a stone."

"I'll go with the horse," Thomas said.

He could see Pop thinking. It was Gallagher's he had in mind, not Sweeney's.

"Ah, Thomasy, you need your sleep, every bit of it. Look at you. You look like a beanstalk back in Granard."

"There's fighting going on at Gallagher's," Thomas said. "Bare-knuckle fighting in the back room. It's against the law, you know that. Even to watch."

"Ah, but I'm going to the stable, to Sweeney's, remember?" Pop's eyes slid away from him.

Thomas swallowed. There was nothing he could do. He listened to Pop's footsteps on the way down the stairs, then took the bag with his clothes from the living room and slid it under the bed in the lighthouse room. Then he heard the sound of voices.

He'd read about old houses with ghosts, but this house wasn't that old, maybe thirty years or so, and he wasn't afraid of ghosts; they were just dead bodies over in Holy Cross or Green-Wood Cemetery. His mother might even be one if she was there. He'd tried to ask Pop more than once, but Pop was hard to pin down. He'd look up at the ceiling, or remember he had something to do in another room, or even whistle a bit of a song.

The sounds were coming from the heat register. He stared at the curlicued iron covering the rectangular space in the floor, and heard something again. Was it laughing? Coming from the apartment downstairs?

He spread himself down on the floor, with his ear on the cold metal. It sounded like the surf crashing onto the shore, not that he'd ever seen the ocean, but he could imagine it from all the books he had read about it.

He heard the girl's voice then.

Bird.

A good name for her. She wasn't a sparrow or songbird, though. She stood so straight, and her face was strong. He thought of her trying not to laugh, but it had bubbled out of her anyway. He'd put her in one of his stories; he'd do that this week.

He wanted to know what the mother's name might be. He'd find out tomorrow. How wonderful to have a mother with a face like that, with those kind eyes. And the daughter was going to look just like that one day.

What else did he know about them? A father who worked on the bridge, she had said, a brother, and a sister who loved to cook. As hard as he pressed his ear against the register, he couldn't hear what they said, only the sounds, deeper for the father or brother, lighter for the women.

He threw himself on the bed. It was hot in there, the air stale, but he was tired; he'd gotten up early to pack and sweep out the old apartment. His stomach growled. Always a bit of hunger there. But he fell asleep thinking of Bird, and the rest of that family downstairs.

CHAPTER FIVE
{BIRD}

On Monday morning, Mama bustled around dropping potatoes in one pot to boil, and eggs in another. "We'll put them on ice before we leave, and have a cold supper on this hot night."

"And Annie will be sure to make us a pie." Bird hummed as she snipped off a couple of aloe shoots for old Mrs. Cunningham's legs. They were going to her apartment at the other end of Water Street to bathe her and make her comfortable.

It was quiet in the kitchen, peaceful. Da slept in the bedroom after the graveyard shift at the bridge, Annie was at the factory banging slabs of wood into boxes, sometimes banging purple blisters into her fingers, and Hughie had taken the ferry over to Manhattan before any of them were awake, to work at the market.

She folded the sharp green aloe shoots into a piece of

paper and tucked it into Mama's bag, then piled up the old newspapers to take down to the ash cans in the areaway.

"You're happy today, Bird," Mama said from the stove.

"I like going to Mrs. Cunningham's after all."

Mama raised her eyebrows. Mrs. Cunningham had a miserable disposition, slapping out at them as they combed her hair or rubbed cream into her hands, complaining that the bed was too lumpy, the covers too heavy. But Bird was strong enough to lift her now, to straighten the tangle of sheets under her, and when they were finished and she was clean and the bed neat, Bird had a feeling of satisfaction.

"If only she didn't act like a scalded cat," Bird said, thinking of the scratch on her arm from last week's visit.

Mama spread out her hands as if she were smoothing down Mrs. Cunningham's lumpy bed. "I'd be complaining, too, if I'd been in bed for ten years with only my rosary beads to keep me company."

They drained the potatoes and eggs and rested them on top of the square of ice in the box. Mama tiptoed into the bedroom to lean over to kiss Da without waking him, and Bird reached for her hat.

Moments later they started down the stairs, both of them glancing up at the Nearys' closed door.

"Tell you what, Bird. When we're finished later this morning, go upstairs and knock on the door. Take the boy around. Show him the neighborhood."

"That's not a good idea." How embarrassing to go up there and knock, and worse, walk him around, the mess of him, for everyone to see. "I don't think he's touched a washcloth to his face since the day he was born."

Mama tilted her head. It was hard to say no to her.

"All right. I guess I could do it for a while."

"Ah, Birdie, that's my girl."

Water Street was busy this morning, carts in the street with stacks of walleyed fish, and stands with blue-legged crabs, still alive and scuttling around on small hills of chipped ice. "I'm glad we're having eggs," Bird said.

They stayed with Mrs. Cunningham all morning, chasing the dust out from under her bed, washing her poor old body, and at the end Bird twisted Mrs. Cunningham's long hair into two smooth braids.

"Silver," Bird said. "Pretty."

For the first time, Mrs. Cunningham smiled, showing toothless gums. "In my drawer there's a flower," she said. "You can have it."

Bird began to shake her head, but Mama was nodding, so she opened the drawer and took out a small pink paper rose. "I love it," she said, and tucked it in her pocket.

And then they were outside in the heat, walking slowly. "You have a way with the patients, Bird," Mama said.

Back at home, they climbed the stairs to the apartment. She'd really have to do a better job on the sweeping Saturday, Bird thought, glancing at the drifts of sand in the corners of the steps. But right now she was ready to sink down at the table for a cup of tea with three teaspoons of sugar, and a bit of Annie's leftover yeast cake.

Mama nudged her. "The poor boy has probably been up there all morning without anything to do."

Bird stifled a sigh and gulped down the tea. She went out on the landing, still savoring the last bite of cake. But before she could even climb the stairs to the fourth floor, he came down, almost as if he'd been watching for her.

"I saw you and your mother go out a while ago."

Yes. He'd probably been peering out the door for an hour.

"What's her name anyway?" he said.

Why did he want to know that? "Nora. My father calls her Nory."

They went down the steps. Sullivan the baker was in the window, a smudge of flour on his nose. "Watch." She waved at him.

The baker paid no attention.

"See? He's the crankiest person in all of Brooklyn."

Without saying where they were going, she walked with Thomas toward the school a few blocks away, and pushed open the door. "Just a couple of weeks left before it starts again." She peered down the hall to be sure the janitor wasn't around to chase them out. "Come on."

They went to the end of the corridor and down the stairs. Strange to go downstairs when they wanted to go up, but the only door they could use to get to the roof was in the basement. It led to a dusty stairway that had the janitor's footprints etched on its steps. Halfway up, she pointed out a huge gray cobweb that drifted across the corner of the wall. A memory: *"Help me, Da, I just walked into a spider's house."*

"Ah, Bird, lucky for the spider. But they build bridges, don't they? Look, the line joins one side of the doorway to the other."

Thomas pushed against the heavy door and stood back to let her go first. Better manners than anyone else around, she had to admit, and remembered the woman in the picture, Lillie. Had she taught him?

Outside was the roof with its ashes and dust scattered across the tar. They edged their way to the wall and leaned over to peer down. Laid out in front of them were the streets of Brooklyn, some of them straight and even, others curved.

Thomas was so far over the edge, she took a step closer, thinking to grab his arm before he tumbled down all that way. She looked at his shirt, same one as yesterday, and probably last month, if the truth were told.

She pointed at the doctor going along the street below, sitting up high in his carriage, his horse the most beautiful gray in the city. "Mama says he gets less sleep than she does," she said, "and she hardly sleeps at all."

She watched until he turned the corner and then looked up toward the bridge towers: the one on their side was finished, the one on the other side a place of furious activity, workers going up and down on ropes, trying to finish it by next year.

She was beginning to see how the bridge might span the river, people going back and forth, and Da had said there was even room for railroad tracks.

"It will change everything for us," he'd said. "People will be able to go to work in the city, to shop." He smiled. "Brooklyn and Manhattan are reaching out to touch each other."

And then, so much like Da, he'd said, "But what I picture, what I love to think about, is that right here at our doorstep, we'll have the most beautiful bridge in the world. And that's something, isn't it?"

She glanced down at Water Street now, and leaned closer to the edge. She drew in her breath. Was that Hughie down there? "What is it?" Thomas asked.

She was glad he didn't know Hughie. Glad he didn't know that Hughie was supposed to be working, and why wasn't he? Instead he was standing in a group on the corner with members of that gang, Sons of Sligo or whatever its name was.

His arms were waving. What was he talking about? But she could guess. It was about fighting, about boxing with his bare knuckles, the Irish against the Yankees.

Da would say, *We're all Americans now.*

And Mrs. Daley with her biscuit-dough arms folded over her huge chest, her elbows poking out of the raveled sleeves of her sweater, had said more than once, "It's the good-lookers like Hughie Mallon who give you problems, fighting and carrying on. Ah, his poor mother, who knows what will happen to him? He's looking for trouble."

Bird didn't want to think about it. "Do you know why they began the bridge?" she asked in a rush.

Thomas stared at her with that intent look he had. Whatever she said might be written in his notebook. "Sometimes in winter," she began, "the ice is so thick the ferry gets caught in it."

Thomas glanced toward the river that rushed along, blue and then suddenly gray as the clouds moved over it. "Black water against the white floes. I can see it."

"One day a man named John Roebling was in a hurry to

get from Brooklyn to Manhattan," she said, "but the river was packed with ice, one piece crashing into another. And finally—"

Thomas raised his hand. "The ferry was caught."

"Yes. And Roebling told his son, 'I'm going to build a bridge, and people won't have to take the ferry on a winter day.' "

He pulled at her sleeve. "See that group down there?"

She pretended she hadn't heard. "Before he could build the bridge, his foot was smashed against the dock pilings. He died of lockjaw. Bad luck for the son, too," she said. "He got the bends from going down in one of the caissons deep under the water. He's an invalid over on Hicks Street."

Thomas's eyes were still on the group on the street.

"He watches from the window with a telescope while his wife, Emily, finishes the bridge. A woman, can you imagine?"

Thomas pointed. "Do you know who they are?"

She twitched her shoulder.

"That one with the dark hair, waving his arms?"

"Why do you want to know?"

"Just wondering."

She hesitated. "That's my brother, Hughie."

CHAPTER SIX
{BIRD}

She could hardly wait to walk back home with Thomas. Once there, she stood at her doorway watching until he disappeared upstairs, and then she was out again, feeling beads of perspiration on her forehead and down her back from the heat. She ran full tilt into Willie, the baker's assistant. "Sorry," she called over her shoulder breathlessly.

She passed the school and went to the corner looking for Hughie. Only one of the group was still there. "Have you seen my brother?"

"And he would be?" How fresh he was. He knew very well who it was. "Hugh Mallon."

Hugh Mallon, who was supposed to be working, and wasn't. Hugh Mallon, who was fighting whenever he could in a city where it was against the law. Hugh Mallon, whom she loved best.

The boy pointed. "Isn't he supposed to be working at the market?"

"He certainly is."

"Well then—" He waved toward the ferry.

She went past, thinking about stepping on his boots, and close enough that he had to step back. She turned the corner toward the ferry.

She caught up with Hughie a block before the terminal. She called out, and he turned, smiling. The anger went out of her. There was something about his face, those blue eyes like the sky on a summer day, that she loved the look of. It reminded her of being so little she'd have to take big steps to keep up with him. It reminded her of one night when she was sick and he'd brought her home an ice from the sweet shop, lemon and tart.

"Oh, Hughie," she said now. "What are you doing?"

"Doing?" he asked. "Delivering fruit to one of the big houses on Hicks Street."

Did she believe him? But he never lied.

"What about—" she began. "I saw—"

He tucked her arm in his. "We'll stand by the water and take in the breeze. What could be nicer on a hot day? And old Mr. Breslin at the market won't mind if I take a little longer getting back."

They leaned on the railing. The water was smooth as silk on this breathless day. What could she say to him?

She remembered the last night he had worked on the bridge, months ago now. She'd heard the sound of heavy footsteps on the stairs and heard the door bang open so hard it slammed back against the wall. Da and two of Hughie's friends carried him inside, putting him on the couch, his knees bent to his chest, his arms twisted.

"What is it?" Mama said as Bird backed away to stand in the corner near Hughie's head, hearing his moans. Tears ran like white rivers on his filthy face.

Hughie crying.

Da shook his head. "He was deep under the water working in the caisson."

The caisson. Bird hated the thought of it. A huge box, a block long, that had been sunk all the way down to the riverbed, the bottom open to the sand and boulders. Inside that caisson, in the yellow glow of lanterns, in that suffocating air, Hughie had been digging away those huge rocks so the bridge tower could be laid.

And now, the dreaded caisson disease had come to Hughie.

"When he climbed the ladder to come out," Da said, "he couldn't straighten. He rolled on the street with the pain of it."

Mama stood there helpless. "My own son," she said. "And I don't know what to do."

"No one does," Da said, hovering over him all that night and the next day, until at last the pain eased and Hughie was himself again, lucky to be alive.

"You don't have to go down there ever again, Hughie, no matter what," Da had said.

Hughie had held up two fingers and she knew what he meant: the two dollars a day that he brought home for the farm box would be gone forever. How little he'd make at the box factory or the market.

"What are you saying?" Hughie asked now.

"Why are you fighting?"

He turned to her. "I'm not fighting. I'm standing here with my favorite person in the world, looking at the water, wondering what it would be like to be on that boat over there." He pointed. "On my way out west."

She squinted in the sunlight, looking at the spanking sails of a boat gliding down the river. She looked back at him. Once, two or three years ago, they had taken the ferry to Manhattan. He'd held her up to see the houses and the church steeple as they chugged away from Brooklyn. "Don't let me fall," she'd said, grasping his hair.

"Ah, never," he'd said.

"Remember—" she began, reminding him of that misty spring morning, and he nodded, smiling.

Later she realized he'd distracted her. She hadn't said the things she wanted to say. She hadn't said any of them.

CHAPTER SEVEN
{THOMAS}

All week it had stormed, with rumbles of thunder vibrating through the apartment. Pop had gotten a job down near the bridge, weighing loads of granite as the horses brought them in. Thomas wondered how long this job would last. But it was Sunday now, and Pop would sleep most of the day.

The rain had finally stopped. From the window he saw wisps of steam rising off the roof across the way. Everything was wet, sticky.

He went to the door, propped it open, and sat there leaning against the stairway and writing in his notebook. It was the coolest spot he could find, with that small breeze coming up the stairs.

He looked down to see the mother, Mrs. Mallon, starting up the stairs. She was wearing a hat with a veil and had a missal in her hand. Coming from Mass, he thought.

Did she think he was spying on them, sitting in the stairwell over their heads?

Of course he was spying, he knew that. He hadn't seen Bird in a couple of days; he hadn't seen any of them, but he told himself that even if it got to be two hundred degrees in that apartment, he'd keep the door shut from now on. He would have closed it, but Mrs. Mallon had already seen him. He waved the book in front of his face. "It's hot up here."

"Come down and have Sunday dinner with us." She pushed her veil back over her hat. "It's Bird's birthday, and you haven't met the rest of the Mallons yet."

He almost said no, but stood up and went down the stairs.

They were all crowded into the kitchen, Bird looking at him over her shoulder at the counter. An older girl called, "I'm Annie, and I know you're Thomas." The fighter sat on the edge of a cot in the corner, a newspaper hiding his face, but he waved one arm at Thomas.

Who was left? A gray-haired man: the father. He had a good face, a face for a story. And another woman was stirring something in a pot. She looked just like Mrs. Mallon, but her nose turned up the slightest bit. "I'm Aunt Celia," she said.

There wasn't enough room at that small table with one end against the wall. Thomas counted the chairs, two on each side, and the fifth on the other end.

It didn't seem to bother anyone. The bowls went on the table, and the fighter, Hughie, folded the newspaper behind him, reached over for another bowl the older sister had filled for him, then moved to make room for her on the cot.

The stew was thick, filled with carrots and potatoes and shreds of lamb, and Thomas felt the first mouthful all the way down.

He took a quick look at Hughie then. He had bruises on his face and knuckles.

Mrs. Mallon waved at him. "You're lucky today, Thomas. They left you a place at the table. Usually everyone fights for it."

He could feel his face get hot. He shouldn't be there, but there was nowhere he'd rather be. The small room was steamy with all those people, Mr. Mallon saying grace, then knives and forks clinking and everyone laughing at a story the aunt was telling about a goat in Ireland.

"Ah," said Mrs. Mallon. "Remember that goat, so stubborn with its yellow teeth, butting at us whenever we tried to cross the field?"

Mr. Mallon smiled. "Strange, isn't it? We couldn't wait to get out of Ireland, and now all these years later, what we remember is not the starving but the living."

They were all quiet; then Mrs. Mallon spread out her hands. "All of us scattered now. My brother Patch working on a farm in New Jersey, Maggie and Francey out west—" She hesitated. "Parents long gone."

"Ah, Nory," the aunt said, "we can't be sad on Bird's birthday."

Thomas looked down at his plate, pretending he belonged there with them, that he knew all about their family. Then Pop's face was in his mind. How would Pop feel if he knew Thomas wanted to be part of this family?

He swallowed. Pop was just upstairs sleeping, and Thomas would never leave him, even if he could change things around and be part of the Mallons. But thinking about it, for just that second, that he was one of them, that he really belonged there, gave him a rush of warmth in his chest.

Bird nudged him. "What's that look on your face? Have you swallowed wrong or something?"

He didn't have time to answer. He heard footsteps, someone running up all those flights. There was a quick knock on the door and then it flew open.

The man standing there was familiar. He delivered milk in the mornings in a faded cart with a skinny gray horse.

Everything stopped: forks half raised, a bowl being passed. It seemed that the man was bathed in red, great swaths of it across his shirt and hands. And then Thomas realized: he was covered in blood.

The man reached out to Mrs. Mallon, who was bending already to pick up her bag. "You're cut," she said.

"Please, Mrs., hurry," he said. "It's not me. It's my son."

Bird stood too, pushing the table back, plates and bowls rattling. "I'm coming."

What could have happened to cause all that blood? Thomas couldn't stop staring at the man and listening as the three of them went down the stairs.

CHAPTER EIGHT
{BIRD}

Mama and the milkman flew down the stairs in front of her, their feet barely touching each tread. "I can't get the doctor," he said breathlessly.

Bird knew that was so. She had seen the doctor earlier, his carriage rattling along the street so fast that people hardly had time to get out of the way. "Just a block," the man said. "A block."

Bird stumbled and ran to catch up with them. How quiet everything was this Sunday afternoon, how still. No horse and wagon clopped down the street, no cart; no one stood on the corner talking. It was as if they were the only ones in the world. Their footsteps echoed, and Mama's breathing was heavy as they hurried toward Fulton Street and up the steps into the house.

"Fifth floor," he said. "I'm sorry."

Mama waved her hand to tell him it was all right, but she

held her side as they took the long flights up. Bird wondered what they'd find at the top of those stairs, what terrible thing, and then there was a quick memory of the milkman standing at their door once, his face like an apple that had browned and lost its juice, complaining that they hadn't paid the bill on time.

The door to the apartment was half open. It smelled as if no one ever opened a window in there. There must be a pot of day-old cabbage on the stove. The shades were down, and she stumbled over someone's coat bunched up on the floor.

"The bedroom," he said. "In the bedroom."

"Go back out, Bird," Mama said. "Sit on the steps in the hall."

So what did you do? Annie might have said later. *Sit outside in the hall?*

She gritted her teeth so she wouldn't gag over the smell. She thought of the baby, Mary Bridget. "I can help, Mama." She tried to keep her face smooth. "Really."

Mama didn't bother to answer but went straight into the bedroom, where there was no window and almost no light. It felt as if it were the middle of the night—worse than that, because at home Mama always left a candle burning in a bowl in the kitchen.

"I can't see." Mama's voice was sharp. "Get a lamp or a candle quickly."

"Wait." The milkman scurried out of the room. Bird could hear him rustling around somewhere.

A nest of old clothes was piled on the bed, but she couldn't see the corners of the room, and only the shadow of a woman kneeling next to the bed. Bird could hear her own breathing now, almost as if she were deep under water.

The man came back with the lamp flickering in his hand, holding it so they could see the bed. Bird's hand went to her mouth. How could there be so much blood?

The boy's eyes were closed, dark lashes curved over his cheeks. His face was the color of old milk. She drew in her breath. She had seen that boy on the street dozens of times, playing ring-o-levio or lined up at the boys' entrance at school: dark hair and eyes, much younger than she was.

Mama leaned over him so Bird couldn't see his face anymore, but just one hand, the fingers curved, blood under the nails and on the knuckles.

Bird backed up against the wall. Even though she'd told Mama she could help, she had no idea of what to do. She didn't want to go near him, didn't want to touch him.

"What happened?" Mama asked. But even as she spoke she was running her hands over his torso, his arms. And to herself: "Where is it? Where is it?"

"I don't know," the man said. "I don't—"

Mama turned the boy over, moving his face so he could breathe. "Ah, there."

In spite of herself Bird leaned closer to see a great flap of skin open across his scalp.

The woman drew in her breath, sobbing. "Your fault," she said to the man. "Raging and smashing that bottle, leaving it for him to fall over."

"All right," Mama said as if she were talking to herself, but stopping the woman from saying what she might have said next. "I want whiskey. Do you have—"

The man scuttled away and brought it back as Mama rummaged in her bag. She dumped everything out on the floor, small jars of herbs rolling, clean cloths and pieces of rubber tumbling, and metal clinking. She picked up a scissors, a bottle that held needles, some of them curved, and thick black thread.

"The light," she told the milkman. "Hold it closer." She took the whiskey bottle from him, unstopping it, and poured the liquid over the boy's scalp.

Red washed into pink, and now there was white bone deep inside that flap of skin. She kept pouring until the smell of the whiskey blocked out the other smells in the room, pouring, then leaning over to look inside the wound, and pouring again until there was almost nothing left in the bottle.

She clipped at the boy's hair, then edged the skin together with her fingers, and Bird felt queasy, acid coming into her throat; she swallowed, biting her lip so she wouldn't be sick.

How many times had she seen Annie sew in a sleeve, easing both sides so they wouldn't pucker, taking a stitch, and smoothing out the fabric again? And now Mama was doing the same thing to someone's head. Someone's skin.

All Bird wanted to do was to get out of that apartment and run back home where they'd been celebrating her thirteenth birthday, all of them laughing at Aunt Celia's story, but she wouldn't let herself step back.

"He's waking now," Mama said to the woman. "Hold his head."

The woman scrambled away. "I can't, I can't." She said what Bird was feeling.

Can't.

"Bird, come here."

She hesitated. *Just this time,* she told herself, listening to the woman's sobs, *but never again. Never.*

This was nothing like washing a new baby, having a baby named for her, nothing like braiding Mrs. Cunningham's silver hair into smooth plaits. Nothing like anything she'd ever seen.

Bird moved slowly around the man.

"Hold his chin with one hand, his forehead with the other," Mama said, intent on the boy and barely glancing at her. "Don't be afraid to hold him tight. He's going to feel this. He's going to—" She shook her head, and Bird could see the pity in her eyes.

She put her hands where Mama told her, fingers sliding over the blood, sliding, then gripping as he began to move, trying to get away from them, beginning to scream, thrashing, his legs kicking out.

Bird held his head, her fingers in his ears to hold him fast, in his hair, getting up to kneel on the bed next to him, staying out of Mama's light. She heard someone moaning, and realized it was her own voice.

She clamped her lips together and looked up at the ceiling. A thick crack ran across the plaster like a black river. She told the boy, "Lie still, just lie still, it's almost over."

But Mama kept stitching, knotting, cutting, the needle in and out, until a thick line was there instead of that flap; it was almost like the crack in the ceiling.

Bird began to notice a strange feeling; she felt almost feverish. She was dizzy and there was a buzzing sound deep in her head. She knew she had to take her hands away from the boy and steady herself, otherwise she'd fall against the iron railing of the bed.

She let go of the boy and scrambled back against the wall. She realized Mama was talking to her, but she didn't know what she was saying.

Bird closed her eyes, seeing colors in back of her eyelids, reds and greens. She was going to be sick.

She crawled across the floor, skirt in her way, yanking at it, reaching the door, pulling herself up, then stumbling out onto the landing. She was sick in the hall and down the stairs. Then she was out in the street to take deep breaths until the pounding in her head had stopped.

CHAPTER NINE
{THOMAS}

Thomas was back in his apartment, sitting on the couch. He was thinking about the afternoon, wondering if the fighter had recognized him from that first night at Gallagher's, wondering about the milkman's boy.

He saw that Pop was up and on his way out. Thomas was sorry he'd come upstairs. The rest of them had still been there, sitting in the kitchen, waiting for Bird and Mrs. Mallon, and he could have stayed. But somehow it seemed not right.

It was getting dark now. He'd light the lamp, he thought, and write a little, but then he heard Mrs. Mallon calling from the landing.

He opened the door quickly and looked down at her. There was as much blood on her skirt as there had been on the milkman. "Have you seen Bird?" she asked.

He shook his head and reached back to pull his jacket off the hook. "I'll look for her."

"She's had a hard time this afternoon, that girl of mine," Mrs. Mallon said, shaking her head.

"She'll be somewhere along Water Street near the bridge," he said, surprised he knew that, but sure about it. "I'll find her."

"I'd be grateful," Mrs. Mallon said. "I'll change my clothes, and if you're not back we'll all—"

"You don't have to do that," he said. "I'll find her. I know I will."

He flew down the stairs and out the door, crossing to the bridge side of the street. The tower loomed in front of him, a gigantic shadow against the sky.

She was leaning against the railing at the water. Her shirtwaist was covered in blood, her skirt torn. "Bird," he called, but it was as if she didn't see him.

He went toward her, seeing her hair out of its clips, down her back in thick curls. He caught up to her and reached out, holding her arms, realizing she was as tall as he was, maybe even a little taller. Her face was swollen, her eyes filled with tears.

She shook her head, so he leaned against the railing next to her, watching the water lap against the wooden pilings. Across the river he could see the unfinished tower with its jagged top, almost like a huge broken tooth.

And at last he said, "Was it the milkman's boy? Was that it?"

She wiped her face on her sleeve. "I used to cut up bits

of leaves and stems with Mama, and mix them with honey for the neighbors' sore throats." Her hands were clenched on the railing. She turned her head to face him. "The first time I went with Mama I read a story to a little girl sick in bed."

He wanted to tell her she was beautiful. He wanted to tell her he'd started to write a story about her. He had even called her Eldrida to make her smile. But he wasn't sure she'd want to hear any of that.

"I thought it would be babies, you know?" She reached for a handkerchief in her sleeve. "And helping people. But not like this. Not anything like this. I thought it would be so different."

She straightened her shoulders, and neither of them said anything after that.

They stayed there for a while watching the boats, and the water, and the bridge that might never be finished.

Everything was impossible: Bird and her taking care of people, and even Pop's drinking. And what about what Thomas wanted? That was the most impossible of all.

Fall 1875

CHAPTER TEN
{BIRD}

It was Wednesday morning, the first day of eighth grade, and her last year of school. Mama and Annie were at the kitchen table with her. Hughie was still a huge lump under the covers in his bed in the corner, and Da wouldn't come off the night shift for another hour.

Annie slopped a great spoonful of oatmeal into Bird's bowl.

Bird examined it carefully. "Lumps."

"Didn't I just do you the favor of rolling up your hair?" Annie asked, bumping the back of Bird's head with her elbow.

"Didn't I give you half of the money Mrs. Daley paid me for sweeping down the stairs for it?"

Mama leaned over, a loop of her hair over her forehead. "In the Old Country we'd have been grateful for lumps."

Bird and Annie exchanged a look. They all knew. In Ireland they'd eaten limpets and grass when Mama and Da were young and the potatoes had gone bad. If Bird had food to eat, she wanted to say, it might as well be decent, but she didn't, of course. She didn't have the chance, anyway.

"Where's Thomas?" Mama asked.

Thomas, who had breakfast there now more often than in his own apartment.

"I thought you went for him, Bird," Annie said.

"Not yet." Bird looked out the window at the bridge tower, rosy as the sun caught the edge of the stone. She wondered if seagulls flying by would stop for a rest.

"Bird," Annie said.

"Just go to the stairs," Mama told her. "Give him a call."

Bird raised the spoon to her mouth, closing her teeth to filter the oatmeal like a sieve, then went out into the hall to lean against the banister. "Thomas," she shouted up.

"You're enough to wake the dead," Annie said after her.

There was no sign of him. She knew he was there; he just didn't want her to know he was waiting for someone to ask him to eat with them.

"This is the last time I'm going to call you, Thomas. Then I'm going to march right back into my apartment, slam the door, and you won't even have a taste of this delicious oatmeal that Annie made."

That brought him out. The string from his knickers was missing so the legs were falling down, and his white shirt had never seen the underside of an iron in its whole miserable life.

A fine thing for the first day of the last year of school.

Bird went back to her seat at the table and grabbed her spoon as he slid onto a chair next to her.

Hughie sat up and stretched, his hair tousled. There was a new bruise on his chin. He'd been fighting somewhere again. Bird glanced at Mama, hoping she didn't see it.

"I need an ice pick to eat this oatmeal," Bird said, trying to distract everyone, trying to make Hughie smile.

"We're lucky to have oatmeal, cold or hot," Annie said, echoing Mama.

Bird crossed her eyes at Annie and saw Hughie's eyes dance. She sat back satisfied as Annie spooned cereal into Thomas's bowl.

"Someday your eyes will stay like that, Bird. You'll have to follow your nose everywhere you go," Annie said.

Bird took a few more lumps of oatmeal, digging deep. Annie always put a raisin or two at the bottom. She found four.

"Not bad this morning," she said as Annie slid away from the table. Annie reached for her shawl on the hook and put on her hat, ready to go to work at the box factory.

Bird took a quick look at her plain face, her hands bruised from working on the boxes, and stood up. "Wait a minute, Annie."

She went into the bedroom for the pink paper flower Mrs. Cunningham had given her, and tucked it into Annie's hat brim.

"You're not half bad sometimes," Annie said.

"All the time," Bird said, and took a damp finger to a bit of oatmeal on her shirtwaist.

Someone was coming up the stairs as Annie went down, probably a patient looking for Mama. Bird felt a little tick in the back of her throat. It was hard to breathe when she thought of Mama and her patients; the milkman's boy. How disappointed Mama must be in her.

How disappointed she was in herself.

That day, that terrible day, she had come up the stairs with Thomas, and in the bedroom Mama had helped her pull off her bloodstained waist and stood there, her hands on Bird's shoulders, as she washed her arms and hands. Bird had told Mama then that she could never do anything like that again. That grayish white bone, the blood seeping out—

"This is the way of it," Mama had said, almost sternly. "We've all been through it."

Now Bird bent down to kiss Mama at the table, getting a whiff of the sweet smell of her. And Mama reached up to cup Bird's cheeks in her hands, hands that were rough from washing and ironing and working with her patients.

Bird slid out the door as a woman came in, and looked back to see Thomas shoveling in oatmeal as if he had spent his childhood in the Old Country and this was the first good meal he'd had in his life.

She hurried for the first few blocks. Who knew if he'd try to catch up? The last thing she needed was to have anyone see her walking along with Thomas Neary.

Besides, she'd waited for this day all summer. This was the last year she'd ever spend in school. She'd be fourteen next July, and it would be time for her to go to work.

To work. But not to walk through the streets of Brooklyn carrying a medicine bag of her own.

Would it be the box factory like Annie during the day?

Would it be the fish store or a vegetable market? Or worse, cleaning someone's house?

How could she spend the rest of her life like that, doing something that didn't matter to her? And remembering what Da always said: *"We have to better ourselves in this new country. Each generation doing better than the last no matter how hard it seems."*

There was a spot of pain in her chest like one of Annie's oatmeal lumps. She shook her head, shaking it away as she reached the schoolyard and went in between the great iron gates.

CHAPTER ELEVEN
{THOMAS}

He'd never been to a school like this before. Girls and boys in the same classroom. In the other schools they'd even gone in separate doors.

Strange to see the girls lined up on one side of the room, big bows in their hair like butterflies, nails buffed, looking at the boys from the corners of their eyes.

And all because Brother Anthony, who had taught the boys, had been transferred out to Canarsie at the last minute and Sister Raymond had volunteered to take on all the boys and girls in the eighth grade by herself.

He angled his way around on the boys' side so that he was sitting beside Bird.

Halfway through the afternoon she left a couple of lemon drops on her desk next to her inkwell, and he leaned over to take one, thinking they were there for him.

What a look she gave him, eyebrows almost meeting in

a frown! It made him laugh, leaning over his desk, trying to listen to Sister Raymond going on about the eighth-grade essay. It wasn't even due until June. What he wanted to do with the rest of his life! He could write that in ten minutes.

He looked across at Bird, and she glared back, making him laugh again. *Eldrida,* he wrote on a scrap of paper so she could see it. But Sister tapped her pointer, frowning. "For most of you," she was saying, "it's the last year of school."

For him.

He didn't mind. He could work during the day if he had to, doing anything. But at night! What he wanted to do was write.

He half listened to Sister as he pulled himself up in his seat. He could see the bridge towers outside, and thought of writing about them. It seemed that everywhere he looked there was something to write about.

He thought of the lemon drop, and leaned over to take the second one, but before he could, Bird slammed her hand down on his.

"What's going on back there?" Sister Raymond said, and he looked away.

They worked on geography, on history, and the clock barely moved; then science, and arithmetic. It was all easy for him. At the end of the day Sister read from a thick book—*Great Works of Literature*—and he barely heard the bell. If only he could write someday like Victor Hugo did, or Sir Walter Scott.

They lined up, and he heard one of the girls laughing as she whispered, "She gives him candy. They're probably going to get married."

He turned. Bird's face was scarlet, and he tried not to grin. And when she saw him waiting at the door for her, she looked so angry that even the huge bow on her head quivered. It made him laugh again, and he went ahead without waiting for her. At home he stood on the landing until she opened the door downstairs.

"Cup of tea, Bird?"

"Thomas Neary," she said, "I'll thank you not to take my candy."

"My father left cinnamon buns from Sullivan's Bakery up here," he told her.

"No, thank you."

"Want to see the towers from the window?"

She hesitated. "All right. Some tea and a look at the towers then."

Her voice was almost like her mother's.

He left her in the living room and rattled around in the kitchen. The milk was sour; what was he going to do about that? And the buns didn't look so fresh after all. He made the tea anyway, reached for a plate, and knocked it off the counter, smashing it on the floor into a dozen pieces in his haste.

"What's happening?" she called in.

He looked out the kitchen door. She was running her hands over Pop's leather-covered books. The best thing they owned, they'd been left behind by a tenant in one of their apartments. Pope and Dryden, Edgeworth and Swift.

His opened writing book was on the table. He saw her walk over to it. She'd see the story with Eldrida as the heroine and know in an instant he had written about her. Or maybe she'd read about her mother on her way to a patient, her blue bag over her shoulder, or the scent of dried herbs hanging in bunches from their kitchen ceiling.

He never thought about the picture of Lillie until he was coming into the room with a cup of tea in each hand. There was a story under that, a mother reading poetry first to him and then to an audience.

He took a step closer to Bird and saw the picture, the newspaper clipping. Lillie with pearls the size of marbles looped around her neck. The hat with the feather dipping over her forehead. Beautiful Lillie.

Bird looked a little guilty that he'd seen her peering at the book.

And he felt a sudden flash of something; he didn't even know what it was. He knew the Mallons felt sorry for him, and maybe that was even why Bird was here now. Before he could stop himself he was saying, "She's in London, acting," he said. "Someday soon she'll come back."

He didn't say she was his mother, but he knew that was what Bird thought. He let her think it.

CHAPTER TWELVE
{BIRD}

It was late fall, most of the leaves gone from the trees. And it was almost dinnertime. From the bedroom window, the houses across the yards were beginning to blur into the sky. It wasn't all dark, though. Squares of light flickered from some of the apartments.

Mrs. Daley had forgotten to pull in her wash and the wind had picked up. On the line, her shirtwaist sleeves were puffed out as if her arms were still in them, and her long underwear kicked at the shadows.

As Bird watched the light fade outside, she thought about that eighth-grade essay, even though it wasn't due until the end of the year. How could she know what she wanted to do with her life? All these years she'd thought she'd be a healer like Mama, and now she knew it was never going to happen. She brushed thoughts of the milkman's boy away and thought about the essay.

Writing wasn't easy for her. It wasn't like arithmetic, not like a column of numbers to be added or subtracted from the top of the blackboard to the bottom, neat and organized; or science, figuring out the why of things.

Her mind jumped to another problem. Sister Raymond, her eyes large under those straight dark brows, had said today, turning to look at the class, the crisp white bands under her veil crackling with starch, "Wouldn't it be wonderful," she had said, "if any of us who had a book at home would bring it in to share?"

Ellen Burke immediately said her father had books. Ellen Burke, who had shamed Bird with that talk of candy and marrying Thomas Neary. Bird shuddered, thinking about it.

In the classroom, there had been a chorus of yeses about bringing books. All except for Thomas, who was half out of his seat, looking out the window.

Bird had stared up at the painting of the Alps that hung over the blackboard. She thought of her apartment, filled with Hughie's cot, the table, the stove, the ice box, Mama's dried plants hanging in wispy bunches from the ceiling, and the painted cabinet with the glass doors.

In her mind she had gone through the curtains that led to Mama and Da's bedroom, to the teeny one she shared with Annie. Among all those beds and covers and skirts and coats, the washstand with a sliver of soap and bits of towels draped over the edges, not a book was tucked in anywhere.

Now Mama called from the kitchen. "Bird?"

She stacked her papers, glad not to have to think about

the essay, and listened to Mama's footsteps going from the stove to the ice box. She went down the hall.

"Soup with a bone," Mama said. "Only two shreds of meat on it, but a bone is a bone." She held up five fingers, and nodded for Bird to put the bowls on the table.

Five of them tonight. They could fit at the table. Da had started work early.

Bird gave Mama the best bowl, with the roses in the bottom. Hughie got the plain one because he wouldn't care. Bird wanted the one with the pink flowers on the rim, but she knew it would be nice to give it to Annie, so she took a plain one like Hughie's, and the last one, the one with two chips, was for Thomas.

Mama reached for the bubbling pot on the stove, her hands covered with old rags. "Call up to Thomas," she said. "Call softly."

Bird nodded, but she could make as much noise as she wanted; no one was there but Thomas. If only his mother would come home. He'd be upstairs at his own table instead of waiting for her to call him down.

It was terrible that Thomas's father was over at some pub, sitting on a high-backed stool in front of the dusty window, or stumbling along in the street.

Following in back of Thomas on the way home from school, she had seen Mr. Neary raise his mug to Thomas, pushing open the door with one foot and tossing out a coin, a nickel. At first, she'd thought Thomas wasn't going to reach for it, but he had picked it up and tossed it in the air before he dropped it into his pocket.

"Thomas has a nickel," she said.

"A nickel," Mama repeated. "In Ballilee that would have bought enough greens for a pot of soup I could stand in up to my neck."

If Da had been home, he would have said, *I never saw a pot that size, Nory.* And the two of them would have laughed.

Bird went into the hall. "Thomas," she yelled.

"That's softly?" Annie said to Mama.

Thomas clattered down the stairs carrying a tiny pot of chives. He knew the best way to please Mama.

They sat at the table. Hughie came in at the last minute. He looked at the chives, nodding, and they said grace. "Come, our Lord, and be our guest. . . ."

Bird said a quick amen; then Hugh grabbed one heel of the bread. She took the other, hot to the touch.

"No fair," Annie told both of them. "I was the one who made that bread."

"True for you," Bird said. She tore off a chunk and put it on Annie's plate.

Bird sat there chewing. All of them were there together. How terrible that Mr. Neary spent his time sipping at his pint instead of making his own bread and soup for Thomas, and Mrs. Neary was so far away on a stage somewhere in England.

A beauty called Lillie.

She slid another chunk of the crusty heel onto Thomas's plate. He gave her a quick nod, spread enough lard over the bread to fill a bucket, and wolfed it down as if he hadn't had anything to eat since breakfast. Maybe he hadn't.

Hughie wolfed down his bread too, making loud noises over his soup. Bird knew he was in a hurry to go down to the cellar, where he said he could breathe. He had a punching bag there, and he spent hours pummeling it until his knuckles were red and bruised.

She'd never go down to that freezing cold and dark place by herself. Mrs. Daley had told her a horrible story about it just the other day.

"Hughie," Bird told him, "watch out in the cellar. Make sure you leave the wedge in the door so it stays open."

He wiped his mouth. "Afraid I'll get locked in?"

"What are you talking about, child?" Mama asked, her hand on Bird's arm. "There's no lock on the door."

"Mrs. Daley said—" Bird began.

Mama and Annie shook their heads at each other.

Bird leaned forward. "A woman went down there—"

Hughie polished the bottom of his bowl with his bread. "Go on," he said. "I may be so afraid I won't be able to go past the coal bin anymore, Birdie. You'll have to go for me."

She tried to smile. She was too old to believe Mrs. Daley, but still the rest of the story came out in a fast breath. "The woman was never found. Only her shoes. She had melted clear away like ice on a summer day."

"Ghosts," Annie said.

"That's what Mrs. Daley said. Ghosts of the people who used to live here."

"If I were a ghost," Hughie said, and Bird heard the bitterness in his voice, "would I stay here?" He pushed back his chair.

She raised her voice. "Mrs. Daley said her shoe buckle was so cold it steamed the way your breath does in the dead of winter." But she was talking to Hughie's back as he went out the door.

Bird lifted the spoon for the last sip of soup, and Annie took herself over to sit on Hughie's cot. She picked up her knitting: black wool socks for Da. And soon Thomas went back to his apartment upstairs, saying, "Thanks, Mrs. Mallon," over his shoulder.

"Thank you, too, Thomas, for the chives." Mama pulled herself away from the table. At the counter she poured soup into Da's jar and cut two thick slices of bread. "Why don't you and Thomas go together when you bring Da's dinner down to him?"

"Can't I be alone with Da for two minutes?" Bird said. "Does Thomas always have to—" She broke off.

Mama was looking up at the ceiling as if she could see Thomas going up the stairs through the cracks in the plaster. "He has nothing to do all by himself in that apartment; he'll be happy to go with you."

Bird never had one moment of peace. "He has homework, you know. It wouldn't hurt him to work on his essay." But even as she said it, she knew it wouldn't do any good. And Thomas had probably worked on his writing all afternoon.

And that reminded her. "Why don't we have any books in this house?"

"Books?" Mama said. "Where would we get the money for books? We need money for food, and clothing, and to buy plants for cures." She took a breath. "Most of all we need money to save."

For a farm in New Jersey near my brother Patch. That's what she'd say next.

Bird cut her off. "Books are just as important as food."

Annie began to laugh, rattling her needles. "I'd like to see you go without food for a day, Miss Crow, and then say that."

"Sister Raymond wants us to bring a book to school," Bird said slowly, wondering why she felt like crying.

Mama shut the lid of Pa's dinner pail, then shifted things around in the ice box to make room for the leftover soup. She turned and put her arms around Bird. "You're a good girl, Bird, and you're right, a book is a wonderful thing to have." She smiled. "You might ask Da about it when you go over there."

Bird hugged her, then picked up Pa's dinner pail and went into the hall and down the stairs.

Hughie was still there, just opening the door to the basement. She took a step forward. "Wait," she said. "We never get to walk together. We never even get to talk anymore."

"Ah, Birdie. Didn't you just tell me a wonderful story?"

"I don't mean that."

He waited, his hand on the knob. She saw he knew what she was talking about, that he was quieter every day, and how angry he was just underneath his few words. She had a quick memory of him sitting at the table, head back, laughing. How long ago that was.

"Be the way you used to be," she said. "Walk with me to bring Da his dinner."

She saw him hesitate, and then he shook his head. "Not tonight, Bird."

Annie called down from the stairs, "Did you ask Thomas, Bird?"

Hughie ran his hand over the top of her head and went down into the cellar.

CHAPTER THIRTEEN
{THOMAS}

Thomas wandered through the dark apartment, went from the lighthouse bedroom through Pop's room, and then into the living room to look out the window. Pop wouldn't be coming, though, not for hours.

Thomas went back into the bedroom and sat on the bed, listening to the sounds coming from the register, pretending he was still there having dinner, listening to them talk.

He heard Bird calling. "Want to go down to the bridge with me?"

He grabbed his jacket, flew out the door, and took the steps two at a time. Outside it had begun to rain, a fine mist of a rain: fall leaves were plastered to the walkway, and puddles filled with bits of hay and coal lay in the street. A nice bit to remember for the writing. Water Street! He loved to look at it.

He nodded at Sullivan the baker, who was turning the

key in the lock, and Willie, the assistant, who bent his floury head into his collar for warmth.

He could see that Bird didn't want to talk. She was humming under her breath, hardly paying attention to him.

He heard the clop of hooves in the street behind them and turned to watch the driver snap his whip and shout at the horses. He took a step toward them, thinking about running along in back of the wagon, reaching out to hang on, his feet flying as the horses raced along.

Bird was paying more attention than he'd realized. "Don't you dare hitch, Thomas. I'll tell Mama and she'll never let you come with me again." She looked fierce enough to be a bare-knuckle fighter.

Instead he climbed on one of the iron fences in front of the houses, balancing himself, arms out. He dashed along, grinning back at her.

"You're going to fall off," she yelled, "impale yourself on one of the spikes, and I'll have to roll your bloody body all the way home."

He raised one shoulder. "Would you care?"

"No."

He was laughing again. What was it about Bird that made him do that?

He stood on one foot, just to see what she'd say, but she marched ahead of him, her hair bouncing, her back straight as an arrow.

The tower was up ahead, at the end of the street, fog swirling over the top. He jumped off the fence as she rattled the gate to get her father's attention.

The rain was drenching now. Bird was shivering, her

shawl soaked through. He reached out to take Mr. Mallon's dinner pail from her and was surprised that she didn't pull away.

Mr. Mallon was inside his small shelter, and in front of him was a fire in an ash can. He threw another slab of wood into the can and came toward them, his hair gray under his blue cap. He unlocked the gate and the three of them hurried to the shelter. It was nothing more than a roof and three walls knocked together, but still it was out of the rain, and the fire in front of them made it almost warm.

They sat on the ground, and Mr. Mallon opened the jar of soup, the heat of it steaming into the air, and took a gulp.

Thomas's mouth watered. Even after he had eaten all that bread and soup at the Mallons' table, he was still hungry. He was always hungry.

Strange, there were times he had gone a day without food, and once even two days when Pop was off somewhere and there was nothing in the house. But now that he was eating downstairs some of the time, it seemed he couldn't get enough.

He picked up a piece of granite that lay in front of them; there was a smooth feel to the face of it, the edges jagged on the sides.

"Ah, there's a story to that one," Mr. Mallon said. "It's from a huge block that was being hoisted up toward the tower as they were finishing the top."

Thomas held the jagged stone to his face, turning it one way and then another.

"The block was so heavy the ropes began to vibrate, and suddenly it broke loose." Mr. Mallon was silent for a moment.

"A miracle that no one was underneath. The block buried itself halfway into the ground."

Thomas tilted his head, trying to think how to put that into a story.

"All that stone came from twenty different quarries." Mr. Mallon squinted up. "Hundreds of shiploads of them."

"Can I have it, Mr. Mallon? A souvenir?"

"Why not?" He held out the jar. "Want a sip of the soup?" he asked. "Or some of the bread?"

Thomas hesitated, and Bird slit her eyes at him, so he shook his head, but Mr. Mallon tore off a chunk of bread and handed it to him. Thomas raised his shoulders at Bird before he took it down in one huge bite.

Mr. Mallon screwed the lid back on the empty jar and put it back into the pail. Then he reached inside for a thick slice of one of Annie's cakes.

Bird grinned. "Hughie and I thought that cake was gone. Mama must have hidden the last piece for you."

"Lucky. One of you would have gobbled it down in a moment," Mr. Mallon said. "How about a piece of this, Bird? Thomas?"

"Mama wants it for you," Bird said.

He divided the piece of cake into three even slivers.

Bird took hers in tiny bites, sucking on the raisins to make it last, but Thomas didn't waste time. He ate his piece, then went out in the rain to look at the piles of stone and tools. In back of him Bird's voice was light and quick, almost a whisper, and after a moment, her father answered. Maybe it had something to do with the book.

He was sure the Mallons didn't have a book, and he and

Pop had all those books upstairs. He wanted to give her one to take to school, but he could see her, back straight: *I don't need one of your books, thank you very much, Thomas Neary.*

He heard banging; it was almost like the noise of a woodpecker he'd seen once in Greenpoint, a *rat-tat-tat* over and over again, but it wasn't a woodpecker, he knew that. He went back to the shelter, hearing Mr. Mallon say, "A nightstick."

It meant trouble, one cop signaling another for help, banging his wooden stick against one of the wrought-iron railings or on the ground. It could be anything. A thief. A fire. Boys in trouble. Gangs fighting.

It could be Bird's brother, Hughie.

Another nightstick took up the sound, until they could hear them for blocks.

Mr. Mallon was thinking the same thing. "Was Hughie home?" He raised his hand to push back his cap, as if it were too tight.

"He was in the cellar after dinner," Bird said. "And I think his jacket was still on the hook."

"Good then." Mr. Mallon handed Bird the dinner pail. "Go home." He walked them to the gate and put his hands on their shoulders. "If he's there, tell him to stay home this night. Tell him I said that."

They hurried down the dark back street, stepping around puddles, black and oily, in the alleyways.

"He's home!" Bird said, almost as if Thomas had said what he was thinking.

He didn't answer. He couldn't.

CHAPTER FOURTEEN
{BIRD}

Hughie would be at the back of the cellar in the small room Mrs. Daley let him use. They'd have to walk through the winding passageway with its storage rooms looking like prison cells, and only the dim light at the end to guide them.

But was he there?

How glad Bird was that Thomas was with her, even though she'd never let him know that. She couldn't get Mrs. Daley's story out of her mind. A woman disappearing with only the buckle of her shoe left to say she had been there.

She couldn't remember ever being in the basement alone. The only times she had gone down there, she'd followed Mama with her laundry basket on one hip, or Da as he brought out the ash cans for Mrs. Daley.

Once she'd gone with Annie, and they'd heard something scurry along ahead of them. "The wind," Annie had said. "Old leaves coming in from the cellar door."

Annie knew as well as Bird that it wasn't the wind. Together, they had seen the gleaming eyes of a rat staring back. His body was long, his leathery tail so close they might have stepped on it.

If Annie hadn't grabbed her hand, Bird might have run. But Annie gripped her fingers so tightly she couldn't move. In one motion Annie reached down with her other hand to pick up a pail and threw it at the creature, which scurried away in the darkness.

Now Bird and Thomas walked the last block. As they came up the steps of the house, Mama rushed out. "I'm glad to see the two of you. Mr. Harris needs me, and I've already sent Annie to find the doctor for old Mr. Magher."

Foxglove for his heart, Bird thought, almost seeing where she had written it in the cure book. But how to do it, how much . . .

"Just go. Tell Mrs. Magher the doctor will be there soon."

Bird was limp with relief. She didn't have to worry about foxglove or how much of it to give. She tried to get in a word. "Da wants me to tell Hughie—"

"Never mind Hughie. Poor Mrs. Magher is frantic for the doctor."

Bird and Thomas ran in spurts and then slowed down in between to listen for the nightsticks, but all they heard was the tinkling of the piano in one of the bars, and loud voices that spilled out onto the dark street.

By the time they were back home it was late. The streets

were deserted except for a man hurrying home, his head down. Only a few lights from people's apartments were reflected onto the puddles.

And sitting up at the top of the stairwell, his head resting on the banister, was Mr. Neary. "Ah, Thomas," he said. "There you are. It's late, and you have school tomorrow, don't you?"

"I'll be right up, Pop. Go on in awhile." Thomas turned to Bird, his face flushed. "Do you still want to go down to the cellar?"

Upstairs Mr. Neary began to sing under his breath.

"Don't worry," she said. "Go upstairs, it's late."

Thomas put his hand on her arm. "You know Hughie's not down there."

"He is!" She shook his hand off.

"I'll go with you then."

"Go upstairs, Thomas Neary," she said. "I don't need you. I don't even have to go down there. Hughie's probably in bed."

Thomas looked undecided, but then he went up the stairs and helped his father inside.

She waited until the door was closed, then, heart pounding, opened the one that led downstairs. The wooden steps were unsteady; she could feel them give as she stepped on each tread.

She peered into the darkness. "No lights down here," she said in a matter-of-fact voice, as if Hughie would be sitting in the dark and she weren't afraid. But her hands were damp.

Why was she doing this? She was almost sure he had

thrown his hat into a ring somewhere. She was almost sure he'd be fighting, picking up money that people threw at him as they watched him beating someone, or being beaten himself.

And she was sure of something else. Someday he'd be caught and sent to prison. He couldn't get away with breaking the law forever.

Something moved in the darkness. She banged her hand against one of the wooden storage bins. "Hughie," she yelled.

She was almost crying, breathless, wanting to go back, knowing she should go back, but she was halfway to that little room that Hughie used, and maybe the door there was closed so she couldn't see the lamp.

She passed the window high up in the wall, dust-covered and filthy, but a little light from the street came through. She took another few steps and then began to run toward that room, hitting her knee on something, calling the whole while.

And then her hand was on the door, pushing it open to darkness. "Hughie," she called, even though she knew he wasn't there, probably hadn't been there all night.

She wiped her face with her sleeve, feeling the dampness of it from the rain.

"I hate you, Hughie," she said, and then she started back the way she'd come, almost like a blind woman. She was glad she'd left the hall door open, because she could see the steps ahead of her, and the light beaming down.

Holding up her skirt, she pounded up the steps, and at

last she reached the hall. She stood against the wall, swallowing. Then she went up to the apartment, hoping that Hughie was there, asleep on his cot against the kitchen wall.

But inside, everything was still. She stood at the kitchen door listening. How strange it was not to hear someone talking, how strange that everyone was gone and she was completely alone.

Annie had made a brack for breakfast. The smell of the bread filled the kitchen. Ordinarily Bird would have cut the tiniest edge for herself, but now she couldn't even look at it. There was an acid taste in her mouth.

She went into the bedroom she and Annie shared.

She could almost see Hughie's face in front of her, the stubble of whiskers on his chin, the dark hairs of his eyebrows, the Mallon eyes. She swallowed. "What's going to happen to you?" she said aloud, as if he were right there.

She yanked off her shoes and peeled down her stockings. She'd probably tracked mud down the hall, but she didn't go back to wipe it up. She threw herself into bed with the covers up to her nose, and listened to the creaks of the floor.

Turning back and forth during the night, she dreamed of Hughie, blood coming from his nose, and the new bridge falling, falling.

She heard the door open as one by one they came in: Annie sliding into bed next to her, Hughie in the kitchen, and then at last Mama.

CHAPTER FIFTEEN
{THOMAS}

Thomas helped Pop into his bedroom, giving him a little push so that Pop fell across the bed, asleep. He undid Pop's shirt collar, and his shoes, and stood there, waiting to be sure he wasn't going to open his eyes again.

Then he went to the apartment door and looked down. Bird was coming up the stairs. He knew she'd been in the basement. He could see by her face she hadn't found Hughie. Of course she hadn't. Where was he?

Thomas took a look back at Pop's bedroom and waited until Bird had closed the door. He went down the stairs and let himself out. It had stopped raining but there was a cold wind coming through the streets; everything looked closed, doors shut, curtains pulled over windows. Almost winter. Thomas put his chin down to feel the warmth of his jacket collar.

He'd start at Gallagher's.

A cop was on the corner of Fulton, and he waited until the officer turned down one of the side streets. Had he been one of the ones banging out that trouble earlier? If the policeman had seen Thomas, he would have been sure to ask what he was doing outside at that hour of the night. And what could Thomas have told him? That he was used to going after his father, and this wasn't much different. The cop would have sent him home with a smack of his nightstick across Thomas's arm.

Gallagher's seemed quiet, the lamps flickering into the empty street, and only a few men were on the bar stools inside. He went around the back; light was spilling out from the window into the garden. Hughie was sitting against the tree trunk just as Thomas had the day he and Pop moved to Water Street.

Thomas wasn't sure what to say. He didn't know if Hughie would be angry that he was looking for him. But Hughie moved over a little to give him room.

Thomas wanted to say how cold it was there, the dampness of the earth coming through his clothes, but instead he sat there quietly watching Hughie run his hand over the bark of the tree and then the wet grass.

"Strange," Hughie said. "In Ireland my mother and father had it all, fields, and water running over rocks in the stream. They had a goat, and a pig, and hens. Wouldn't that be paradise if you could have it?" He shook his head. "If only the potatoes hadn't failed."

Pop had told him about that, the vegetables sold to pay the rent, and a field of wasted potatoes, black and oozing, so they were all starving.

"And over in New Jersey there are farms to be had and food to be grown, but not enough money in my pocket to get where I belong." He stared at Thomas. "What am I telling you this for? Don't say a word about my babbling to Bird, will you?"

"I won't," Thomas said. "Of course I won't."

They sat there for a while; then Hughie shook his head, so Thomas asked, "Did you lose?"

Hughie reached into his pocket and pulled out a thin roll of dollar bills. "I won this time, but not by much." He patted the money. "There's something I'll do with this someday, but it'll take forever."

Thomas nodded uncertainly. "Did you hear—"

"The nightsticks? Someone told me about them, but I was busy." Hughie held up his fists. "Somehow we didn't get caught."

There was an expression in Hughie's eyes that reminded Thomas of something, but he couldn't think of what it was. "Do you think you might want to go home now?" he asked.

"You're watching out for me," Hughie said, "is that it? A string bean like you?"

And because Hughie was so much like Bird, Thomas nodded. "That's it. Your father was worried. Bird even went down the cellar looking."

Hughie put his head back. "No one in the world like my sister Birdie." It almost seemed as if he smiled. "Birdie in the cellar. Glad she didn't melt away."

"Me, too," Thomas said.

He helped Hughie up, and they went through the streets together, watching out to be sure the cop wasn't walking along Fulton. Thomas was glad to see the front door ahead of them; he couldn't keep his eyes open much longer.

It wasn't until he climbed into bed that he thought of that look in Hughie's eyes again. And then he remembered. Bird had had the same look the day she'd come back from helping the milkman's son.

CHAPTER SIXTEEN
{BIRD}

The sun was shining the next morning. Bird didn't want to think about being in the cellar last night. And Hughie was safe in bed now. She wasn't going to worry about him today. She was going to think about school.

She pinched her cheeks for color, taking her time, waiting for Da to come home, excited because he'd told her she'd have a book to take with her to school. And something else: "Annie," she yelled into the kitchen, "how about that blue ribbon?"

"I'm wearing it."

"Not that one. The wide one."

"It's brand-new," Annie said, but Bird knew it was all right. She pulled at the ribbon, which was looped over the bedpost, and went to the mirror to tie it in her hair.

Bird threaded her fingers into the grosgrain ribbon, fanning out the bow, and heard the door open. Da was coming in after his long night at the bridge. "Where's our Bird?" he asked.

She went into the kitchen and tapped Annie's shoulder to thank her. Annie looked—Bird tried to think of what it was. Less plain? Almost pretty? Had she seen a boy at the box factory she liked?

"You haven't left then, Bird." Da smiled. "I rushed to catch you."

He beckoned to her, shrugging off his greatcoat and leaving it on the bottom of Hughie's bed—Hughie's arm hanging over the side. Bird followed him into the bedroom.

"Next to all of you," Da said, "this is the most precious thing I own." He pulled aside the closet curtain and reached up to the shelf to take down a package that was wrapped in flowered cotton.

She watched as he unwrapped it carefully. The book!

He touched the leather cover. "I'll tell you about this—"

Mama called from the kitchen. "You'll be late if you don't hurry, Bird."

Da shook his head. "This is more important." He sat on the edge of the bed. "Long ago, Mama and I came here on a terrible ship. It was leaky and rode low in the water. We lived through a storm where the waves crashed over us. Mama's grandda died on that ship."

Martin Ryan.

He sighed. "All those weeks I never believed we'd reach shore." He tried to smile. "Sometimes in life you have to do the hardest things to get somewhere—to change your life." He reached out to touch her cheek.

How often she had heard those ship stories when Aunt

Celia came to visit: no place to wash, lice in their hair, bugs in the lining of their clothes, clothes that never dried, sores from the salt water on their arms, their faces.

Da paused, and when he began again his voice was thick. "For most of my life I had been hungry. But I thought if I could read, I wouldn't mind it so much."

It was hard to look at him, so she looked down at the book instead. How beautiful it was: the title, *Aesop's Fables*, splashed across the cover, the pages' edges dipped in gold.

"A little girl on the ship gave it to me," he said. "Can you imagine? Her family had so much money they could give away a book. It took me years to read it, but I kept at it, and now I know most of it by heart." He smiled. "My brothers, Liam and Michael, would be surprised to know that."

Bird wanted to reach up and touch his face. She thought of him bent over the book, learning it by himself. Years. And all this time he'd never seen his family in Ireland again. He'd had only one letter, which someone had written for his brother Liam, saying that their mother had died, that Liam was back in their old house, and that no one knew where Michael was.

"I look at the three of you, and I want you to have more than we had." He curled his hands into fists. "You have to fight to get ahead." He sighed, and she knew he was thinking of Hughie, and that he didn't mean that kind of fighting.

"Take the book to school," he said, "and take good care of it."

She reached out to hug him, and he patted her shoulder.

"We're lucky to have you, Bird. Much more important than a book."

Da and Mama had never gone to school. What must it have been like not to read—not the newspaper, not the signs in Mr. Taglio's boot shop, in Mrs. Zimmerman's dry-goods window?

They wrapped the book in the cloth again. She tore through the apartment, carrying it under her shawl as Thomas came down the stairs.

In her pocket she had a lump of sugar for the police horses lined up in the street. Thomas would have one too. She picked a different horse every day. There were five, so she managed to get all of them in by the end of the school week.

This morning she picked the gray horse with the white spots. Tall, with his head swinging—she could picture his mane flowing in the wind, and her on his back. Did Thomas's mother, Lillie, have a horse? But Bird had no time to think of her now, no time to watch the horse eat, showing his large teeth. She hurried those last few blocks, Thomas in back of her.

She went to her seat, listening to the buzz of excitement in the room. There were books on almost every desk. Sister Raymond looked pleased as she walked up and down the aisles, her rosary beads rattling against the desks when she picked up a book or bent over to read the title.

Across the aisle, Thomas's arms were crossed on his desk; he was staring out the window. She knew he couldn't see the tower without stretching up high in his seat.

He didn't have a book on his desk. Thomas, whose house

held all those books. He'd even begun to ask her to take one of them yesterday, but she had cut him off. Hadn't she heard about borrowing from Mama dozens of times? *"If we don't have something, we do without. We don't want to be beholden to anyone."*

Bird had told him that. She couldn't borrow from anyone outside her family.

What had she said that was so terrible? She had seen it in his face, but he'd only gone back upstairs to his apartment and closed the door.

Now Sister Raymond was near the front of the room, her back toward them. "Where is your book, Thomas?"

He shrugged, still looking out the window. "Forgot," he whispered, not quite meeting her eyes.

Bird chewed on the insides of her cheeks. What was wrong with that *forgot*? In the short time she had known him, he'd never forgotten anything . . . what they'd had for dinner the week before last, the sick people Mama saw, Father Kinsella's sermon on Sunday.

"Remember Aunt Celia brought me that locket three weeks ago?" she'd say.

"Four."

She'd shake her head, but then realize he was right.

He remembered everything. Maybe that was why he was such a good writer. What he remembered he'd put on paper, but it came out different, more interesting, more exciting than she'd ever been able to imagine.

Where was his book?

She had a sick feeling in her stomach. He hadn't heard

Da tell her they had a book. He hadn't wanted to have one if she didn't.

She thought of Thomas and his messiness, his spending time in their apartment. She saw how much he cared for Mama and the rest of them. And sometimes Mama called him a gallant soul.

Sister Raymond was at the next aisle.

How could Bird have a book if he didn't? She slipped Da's book back into her desk, tucking the pink flowered cloth around it. She crossed her arms over the top of the empty desk the way Thomas had, and leaned her head on them.

Winter 1875

CHAPTER SEVENTEEN
{BIRD}

It was early in the morning, darker than usual because the night had been stormy and crumpled brown leaves were plastered against the window. Next to Bird in bed, Annie was breathing lightly, still asleep. Annie had stayed up late last night, making dozens of tiny gingerbread men to celebrate the beginning of winter, and even this morning Bird breathed in the sweet scent of them coming from the kitchen.

She reached for Da's book on the little table and lay there trying to read in the half-light as she kneaded her feet against the blankets. She didn't have to get up for another five or ten minutes, and she savored the warmth of the bed and the story she was beginning.

What had it been like the first time Da tried to read the same page? She could almost see his finger under each word, the whisper of his voice as he sounded out the words to himself. How had he ever done that? It seemed impossible.

And then she realized Annie's eyes were on her. "Sorry," she said.

"You didn't wake me, not really. I was just thinking about how warm it is, cozy."

Bird smiled at her and nodded.

In the apartment upstairs something dropped and rolled on the bare floor.

"Thomas is up," Bird said. "Or Mr. Neary."

A frown appeared between Annie's eyebrows. "Ah, Thomas, and that miserable father of his." She squinted up at the ceiling. "If I ever have a child—"

"You'd be a lovely mother." Bird poked at Annie's foot with her own. "A little bossy, but . . ."

"I'll never even find a husband," Annie said.

"You will," Bird said fiercely. "I know you will."

"Ah," Annie said, "to have a bunch of children, to be home and cook every day." She shook her head. "It will never happen like that for me. I'm not pretty, not even a little. I'll spend my days in the box factory."

Bird reached out and touched her shoulder. "Not true, Annie, don't say that."

Surely someone would see how good Annie was. Bird thought of Mama telling her once, "*I owe what I know about healing to my neighbor Anna back in the Old Country. Annie was named for her. A special name, and both special people.*"

Annie turned to her. "I'm glad to have you alone for a moment, Bird. I've wanted to talk to you about Hughie."

Bird closed the book. She'd lost the warmth of the morning, the feeling of peace. Thomas upstairs with that father of his, Annie sad, and Hughie—

"Something inside Hughie is broken," Annie said.

Bird thought of Hughie, walking with her so long ago, when she was so small she had to skip to keep up; teaching her to button her shoes; Hughie laughing.

"Anything that's broken can be fixed," she said without thinking. She'd heard Mama say that so many times, even though she wasn't sure she believed it.

Annie slid out of bed and turned to face her. "It's you, Bird. You're the one who can find out what's wrong. He loves you best, you know." She leaned over to tap Bird's foot under the covers. "You're the one we all love best."

Bird lay there, savoring what Annie had said, but then thinking of Hughie skipping work, fighting, his face closed and angry.

Just last night they'd been alone in the kitchen. He had stood there in front of Mama's plants, his head bent, his dark hair falling over his forehead so she couldn't see his eyes.

"Hughie, please," she'd said, not even sure how to put it into words. "Remember what it was like before—" She wanted to say before he'd been sick, when he still worked at the bridge, but something stopped her. He didn't answer.

She heard the sound of the upstairs door closing. Mr. Neary was on his way to work, or maybe to Gallagher's for all she knew.

She stood up then, and dressed, thinking about what

Hughie was doing to this family, and how much she too had disappointed Mama even though Mama had never said one word about it.

In school that morning Sister Raymond stopped at her desk and asked her to stay afterward. Bird swallowed. Was she in trouble? She tried to think of what she might have done. But there was nothing. Bird was the first one finished with the arithmetic examples Sister put on the board every day. She'd answered all the science questions from the booklet Sister had given them.

The only thing Sister Raymond might have seen was the strip of cloth Bird wound around her fingers one after another.

Mama had taught her bandaging. "Practice," she'd said, leaning over her. "Do it a hundred times, a thousand times, do it until you have the feel of it with your eyes closed. Not too tight or the fingers will turn purple."

Why did she do it? Why did she bother? She wondered why Mama had even showed her how. Mama knew it was all for nothing, she thought. But she had done it more times than she could count, and was surprised at how smoothly the bandage rolled itself out now.

She thought of Mama going to patients in the middle of the night, tiptoeing out the door so Bird wouldn't wake and be tired at school the next day. And sometimes from the classroom window she saw Mama trudging up the street, head bent against the wind, holding her hat with one hand and her bag with the other.

Now Sister stood up from her desk, looking toward the door. "It's dismissal time."

Everyone else went to the wardrobe for their coats, then shuffled out the door, Thomas glancing back at Bird. She didn't quite look at Sister, who was coming down the aisle. "Bridget?"

Bird took a breath.

"Ah," Sister said, "I'm sorry. I can see that I worried you. There's nothing wrong." She looked at the chalky blackboards. "I'm going to wash these down. Want to—"

Bird took the small pail to fill from the closet down the hall. Sister Raymond pinned back her sleeves and together they made wet swaths up and down the boards. It was a soothing job, sponging the board and leaving clean patches as they went.

"Well, Bird," Sister said, "what about next year? Going to high school?" She tilted her head. "Or following in your mother's footsteps?"

Bird shook her head. How could she say it would be neither one?

"You're a fine student, Bird," Sister said. "I think you'll be good at anything you do." She went to her desk with a rustle of starch and reached into her drawer. "There's something I want to lend you." She handed Bird a small package.

"Mama says never to borrow—"

"Ah, yes, but from your teacher it's different."

Bird knew what it was by the feel of it. A book. She thought back to the day the class had brought in books, and remembered putting hers away.

She could see Sister remembered it too.

Bird wanted to tell her the whole story, that Da had given her the book, that every night she read one of the stories about the fox, or the rabbit. Da had run his hand over her hair as he passed on the way to work the other day. "Ah, Bird," he'd said, "if I had ever known when I was young that I'd have a daughter who could read."

Something had happened to her because of the reading. What Sister Raymond had said once was true. You could learn anything from books, especially if you looked in back of what the writer was saying. The stories in Da's book were about animals, but if you looked closely, you could see they were really about people and why they acted as they did.

Sister Raymond reached out to put a hand on Bird's shoulder. "I didn't have a book to read until I was in the convent."

"I'll be careful of it."

Sister smiled. "Don't I know that?"

Bird ducked her head and went out the door, Sister calling after her, "I have other books for you to read, Bird."

How strange it was to walk home without Thomas two steps in front of her or two steps in back.

She passed the bakery. Then she stopped. Sullivan must be lonely in that bakery, day and night, she thought, without a wife, without a family, only his quiet assistant working all day in the back. Bird waved at him, and held the book tight as she went up the stairs to their apartment.

CHAPTER EIGHTEEN
{THOMAS}

Thomas didn't wait for Bird. If she was in trouble, she'd have her chin in the air and wouldn't want him to know about it. She wasn't in trouble, though. How could she be?

He turned in at the house. He could close his eyes and know what floor he was on just from the smell of things. Sullivan the baker's smelled of bread or buns, Mrs. Daley's of ammonia from cleaning.

He stopped at the Mallons' landing. Sometimes their apartment smelled of one of Annie's stews, or cakes, or the gingerbread men she made that they ate in one sitting. If he were inside, he could walk over to the window and smell the mint, the lavender, and the geranium leaves that grew in small pickle jars.

And then his own apartment. He opened the door, leaving it open a crack so he could hear what was going on downstairs.

He dropped his coat on the table in the living room, sniffing a little. He could smell the dust from those thick purple curtains. If it had been up to him, he'd have yanked them all down and let in the light and the view of the bridge, but Pop liked to run his hands over them, feeling their smoothness, and once he'd seen Pop lean his cheek against them.

Thomas heard the steady drip from the ice box in the kitchen. There'd be a puddle spreading across the floor by now. He wouldn't bother to go in and look for a while. Let it drip itself out.

He went into the bedroom, reached under his bed for his writing book, and sat on the floor next to the register, leaning against the wall. It was quiet downstairs, no rumble of voices, no laughing, but he liked to sit there anyway, picturing them in that kitchen.

He began a story about a small house by the sea. The sister made iced buns and the father worked as a night watchman at the lighthouse. Inside, the kitchen table reflected the daughter's face.

Eldrida's face.

What about the mother? He sat there trying to picture a mother who wasn't Mrs. Mallon. A mother who was really his own mother.

He wondered for the hundredth time, the thousandth time, if his mother had just walked out and left him with Pop after he'd been born. Pop had told him once that as a baby Thomas had cried all night, every night. Pop had said that he'd walked him through the rooms, back and forth, for hours, patting his back, singing songs his own mother had sung to him in Granard.

Thomas had tried to write about it once, but it made him think of so many things he would have liked to ask Pop. Things that Pop maybe wouldn't want to answer; things that Thomas wouldn't even ask. But if Pop had stayed up all night with him, then maybe he wasn't drinking then. And by that time had his mother been gone already? Or maybe she'd been sick and would reach out from her bed for him?

Was she even alive?

In the end he couldn't finish the story, and instead began one about Bird, and then he heard her calling him.

He slid the book under his bed, went through the kitchen, slipping over the water from the ice pan, more than he had expected, and hooked his fingers over his coat in the living room. "I'm coming," he yelled.

She was outside, sitting on the bottom step of his stairway, a package on her lap, looking up at him.

He started down the stairs.

"How about going to Sullivan the baker's with me?" she asked.

He sank down on the step next to her and ran his hands over the stairs. "Did you sweep last Saturday?"

"Yes, of course. But I have more important things to think about." She tapped the package. "Suppose I brought him a couple of Annie's gingerbread men?"

Before he had chance to say anything, she stood up. "Yes, that's what I'm going to do. And you could come with me."

She said it as if she were doing him a favor.

He clattered down the stairs after her, and they went into the bakery, the bells over the door tinkling. Flour was all over the place, a thin dusting of it on the countertop, footprints of it on the floor, and traces on Sullivan's dark hair.

Sullivan looked up at them from under thick eyebrows. He must have been surprised, Thomas thought, to see Bird. They'd probably never bought store bread in all the years they'd lived there.

Bird stood at the counter, standing straight, her head up. He was beginning to see that the straighter she stood the more nervous she was.

"I want to sell you some gingerbread cookies," she said. "Better than any you've tasted in your life."

Sullivan looked shocked as she tore open the package and held one of the gingerbread men out to him.

For a moment he didn't take it.

"Try it," she said.

He bit into it. "I don't buy baked goods," he said. "I sell them."

"You can pay me a little less, charge a little more."

He shook his head, but Thomas could see she wasn't looking at him. She went outside, the bell banging against the door, and called back over her shoulder, "You can let me know tomorrow, or the next day. My sister makes them."

"Your sister?"

"Yes, you know the one—" She tried to think.

He raised his eyebrows. "The one with the flower in her hat?"

Thomas followed her outside. "What's that all about?" he asked.

She turned. "Did you ever look at Annie's hands? At her blisters? I have to get her out of there, out of the box factory."

He looked back at Sullivan. Sullivan had picked up a second cookie and was eating that, too.

CHAPTER NINETEEN
{BIRD}

It was Saturday afternoon. Bird had forgotten her sweeping job this morning. She hurried downstairs and knocked on the door about twenty times until Mrs. Daley finally handed the broom out to her.

Bird went up to the top floor, tiptoeing. She didn't need Thomas outside following her around. She narrowed her eyes at the steps. Not bad at all, no matter what he had to say about them.

She raised the broom and whisked it awkwardly over the banister. How did the dust have time to settle, with all their hands riding up and down it all week?

"Don't you have a dust cloth?" Annie asked from the doorway. "Look how you've scratched the paint there."

"It's Saturday afternoon," Bird said, smiling as she saw that Annie had put the pink flower in her winter hat.

"Don't you have better things to do than give me house-keeping lessons?"

"It would take forever," Annie said, and started down the stairs. "I'm on my way to shop."

Bird gave a few halfhearted swishes with the broom and then went down past their own landing and on to Mrs. Daley's. There was more sand than she'd thought. She swept it all past Sullivan's door, Sullivan who had come up to their apartment the other night, asking Annie to do some baking for him. "Just a tray or two of cookies here and there," he'd said. She smiled, thinking of Annie, the look of surprise on her face, the rush of pink to her cheeks.

Outside there was a thin dusting of snow from last night, almost like the flour in the bakery.

Bird loved this sweeping job. Mrs. Daley paid her whatever she had in her black purse. Half went into the farm box. That was only fair; everyone else gave what they could for the farm.

"Someday," Mama always said, "our own little piece of land." And Da, with his arms around her waist, told her he'd pick cabbages for her, or roses that grew against a rock wall.

And Hughie used to say, "Ma, you'll never leave Brooklyn, you'll never leave your patients."

She'd laugh. "By that time Bird will take care of all of them for me."

Bird stopped. There'd be no patients for her. Now she realized Mama hadn't mentioned nursing to her, not once, since the day of the milkman's boy.

But outside it was crisp, the sun was shining, and she looked up at the sky trying not to see Mama's face in her mind. Instead there was the sweeping money.

She had her own secret savings. It was hard to hide money in that small apartment. Annie was like a broom herself, sweeping up every single hidden morsel she could find. But Bird had fooled her. Whenever she was alone during the week, she'd stand on a chair and drop a penny onto the very top of the kitchen cabinet. Today there'd be another one to roll around and then lie still, waiting for her to scoop it up. Because someday, she promised herself, she'd have enough money to buy her first book.

She took a few steps through the snow to sweep the last of the sand into the street, and moved backward, only to collide with Officer Regan, the street cop. She righted herself and saw the anger in his eyes. "I'm sorry," she began, "really sorry."

"Never mind tilting along like a windmill," he said. "I have to tell you about your brother."

"Hughie." She breathed it. Always Hughie. Always something to worry about.

"I have him down in the station house," Regan said. "His face is a mess. He was fighting, with that gang of his. They knocked someone through a window." Regan lifted his hat to run his finger across the deep red line it had left on his forehead. "Your parents will have to come down for him. And someone will have to pay for the window."

Bird's fist went up to her mouth. She could feel her teeth against her knuckles. His face was so close to hers, she could see the hairs of his beard, black mixed with gray. "I know all about him," Regan said.

Bird wanted to sink down on the dirty ground. *Hughie, dear Hughie.*

The door to Sullivan's opened with the tinkling of its little bell, and Annie came outside. "What is it, Bird?"

Bird shook her head.

"Your brother is in the station house—" Regan began.

Annie raised her hand. "Whatever it is, my father will take care of it." She angled around them, leaving him open-mouthed. Who else would dare ignore him like that?

She looked at Bird. "If it were up to me," she said, "I'd leave him right there."

CHAPTER TWENTY
{THOMAS}

"You have to come for dinner," Annie told Thomas as he passed her on the stairs. "I've made something new for dessert. A crisp with winter apples."

He turned around and followed her into the Mallons' apartment, into the wonderful smell. Pop had gone out hours ago, after telling him that he had the chance for a new job. The old job as a weigher had lasted only a few months.

Thomas sat on the edge of Hughie's bed, leaving the table for the rest of the Mallons.

Bird came in from her bedroom, and then he heard the heavy steps on the stairs. He saw her glance at Annie, and both of them looked toward the door.

Mr. Mallon came in back of Hughie. "Sit down and listen to me," he said. His face was flushed but his voice soft as always, and Thomas could hear the sorrow in it. "This has to be the end of the fighting. You're destroying your mother, you're destroying me."

Thomas wondered how he could slide out of the kitchen without anyone noticing, but Annie put her hand on his shoulder and shook her head.

Bird was taking down the plates and spreading them around the table. He saw that her hands were trembling, and Mrs. Mallon, who was bringing food to the table, had tears in her eyes.

"Bad enough to have to pay for a window—" Mr. Mallon said as they sat.

"I'll pay for it," Hughie broke in. "Don't worry about that. I don't need you to give me money."

"But the disgrace of going down to the station house to bring you home."

"You didn't have to come for me," Hughie said. "They'd have let me out sooner or later."

"Yes," Annie said with bitterness. "You should have left him there to think about things."

Hughie glanced up at her. "You get harder every day, Annie."

"How can you talk to your sister like that?" Mr. Mallon raised his hand and then dropped it on the table.

"I won't talk to anyone." Hughie stood up and his chair went over.

"If you think you're going out this night, you're wrong." Mr. Mallon stepped back to stand against the door. "You won't get past me."

Thomas looked down at the plate Annie had put in his hand. He could feel his heart thumping. What was Hughie going to do? He was younger and stronger than Mr. Mallon and they all knew it.

"I'm not going out tonight," Hughie said. "I just want some peace myself—nowhere to go but this bed in the kitchen and the bit of space in the cellar. I hate it, all of it."

Mr. Mallon stood aside and Thomas listened as Hughie went down the steps. Thomas ate, feeling as if everyone's eyes were on him, as if everyone was wondering what he was doing there. No one seemed to notice him, though.

Mr. Mallon barely touched his dinner. Finally he stood up and put on his cap and jacket. "I'm going for a walk, Nory," he said. "Do you mind?"

"Go." She reached out and touched his arm. "We've been through worse. We'll get through this, you'll see."

Thomas waited until Mr. Mallon was gone; then he put his plate on the counter and slipped out. "Thank you," he said, not looking at any of them.

CHAPTER TWENTY-ONE
{THOMAS}

Thomas had never been in the cellar before. It smelled damp, and as he passed the coal bin, he could smell the dust of it. He went slowly, not sure if Hughie would mind. Hadn't he acted as if he wanted to get away from everybody?

But Thomas thought about being alone. Sometimes that was worse than anything.

He heard Hughie punching at the bag in the small room in back, and then there was silence. He passed the storage rooms, and saw the crack of light at the end of the dark passageway. He didn't want to call out, but still he wanted Hughie to know he was there, so he made sure to bang into the cans that held the ashes from the furnace.

"Is that you, Thomas?" Hughie called, and shoved the door open with his foot.

"How did you know?"

"I thought you'd be along somehow."

A bench stood along the wall, with cracked leather on top, and Thomas slid onto it. Now that he was there he almost felt foolish. There was nothing he could say. But maybe he wouldn't have to. Maybe he could just sit there for a few minutes.

Hughie gave the bag one last punch, then banged it against the wall with his elbow and sank down on the mat on the floor. "Why do I do it? Is that what you want to ask?"

Thomas shook his head. "No, I never thought about that."

"I've thought about it forever. If I were on a farm some-where, working in a field, I wouldn't care how hard I'd have to work." Hughie put his head back against the wall. "Do you know what it was like working in that caisson under the river? Closed in, knowing the water was just inches away, deep underneath." He shuddered. "But I thought if I had the money—"

Thomas swallowed, thinking of what it would be like to write about that, almost suffocating in that place, afraid of the water coming in, but trying to hold on for one more hour, one more day.

"The disease finished me," Hughie said. "I couldn't go back. I knew I might die of it." He spread his large hands. "A coward."

"I couldn't do it either," Thomas said. "Never."

"I think you could," Hughie said. "I think you could do anything you had to do."

No one had ever said anything like that to him. Was this what it would have been like if he'd had a brother? He'd write those words down: *I think you could do anything you had to do.*

He'd remember it when Pop didn't come in for half the night, for when he had to go looking for him.

"Now listen, Thomasy. Isn't that what your father calls you? I'm going to fight until someone stops me, or bashes in my head. I'm going to fight until I get the money for a farm."

"Your mother wants a farm," Thomas said.

"Ma doesn't want a farm, not really. She wants to stay here and do exactly what she's doing."

Thomas nodded. Maybe that was true.

Hughie stood up and punched the bag. "Come on, I'll show you how to do this."

Thomas stood up and tried, surprised at how hard it was. He kept working at it, though.

"Just don't tell my little sister you're doing this," Hughie said. "What a fierce one she is."

Thomas looked over his shoulder. "Do you think I don't know that?"

They both laughed, and after a while Thomas felt the rhythm of it, one fist and then the other, the bag moving back and forth between them, back and forth.

CHAPTER TWENTY-TWO
{BIRD}

Bird was sitting at the kitchen table reading Sister Raymond's book when Annie came out of the bedroom. "Look what I found in the bottom drawer."

It was the cure book. Bird had shoved it in the bottom dresser drawer weeks ago. But Annie was waiting to see how pleased she'd be.

Annie would never be pretty, but standing in the doorway smiling, with the blue shawl she'd just knitted thrown around her shoulders, she must have looked like Aunt Celia had when she was young, and sometimes Aunt Celia was beautiful.

"Thank you," Bird said, as if she'd been wondering where the book was all this time, but that didn't seem enough. "I didn't remember where I put it."

She could feel Mama's eyes on her as she riffled through

it: dill weed, foxglove, garlic and honey for a cough. And on one page she'd written two Irish cures: coal from a turf fire held under the nose stopped sneezing, and praying ten Our Fathers and ten Hail Marys healed shingles, a painful skin ailment.

She read it aloud to Annie, and Mama laughed. "Having the wee folk on your side is supposed to be good for any disease, especially the impossible ones."

Bird could feel the color come into her face: *impossible*.

Mama waited until Annie was down the stairs on her way to do the shopping. Then she pulled out a chair and sat next to her at the table.

"We could do another one," Mama said. "Just in case you change your mind."

It was the closest Mama had come to saying anything to her about nursing in all this time.

She looked up quickly, but Mama went on. "How about onion for bee sting?"

Head down, Bird wrote as Mama told her how it was used: cut the onion until it oozed, and it was the ooze rubbed on the spot that took the sting out.

"The bee probably dies of the smell if he stays around," Bird said, trying to make Mama laugh.

But what good did it do her to know how to take the pain out of a bee sting? What good was it to know that a warm flannel placed on the neck helped the pain of a sore throat?

It wasn't enough. None of it was enough.

Mama's hand was on her wrist.

She felt the tears on her cheeks, and kept staring down at the book, until it seemed as if they'd been sitting there forever.

"I wanted . . . ," she began at last, spreading her hands out.

"Don't you think I know what's in your head?" Mama leaned forward. "We all have doubts. Always."

Bird gave a shake of her head. "I can't."

"What can I say to you, child?" Mama said. "If this isn't what you want, there are so many other things you can do. It's a big world out there; nothing's impossible. It's not like the Old Country, where we spent our days searching for food, when that was the only thing on our minds from the time we awoke in the morning until the sun went down in the sea."

Bird closed her eyes. She had a quick picture in her mind of Mama walking through the streets, the medicine bag over her arm. "I'll never know enough."

Mama sighed. "None of us will ever know enough, and some problems can't be cured. We just have to do the best we can—"

There was a quick rap on the door.

Mama didn't let go of her hand. "I will tell you this, Bird. I will never be disappointed in what you do. But I think you have a wonderful way with patients. I think—"

The knock came again.

"Thomas," they said together. Bird had completely forgotten she had promised to walk to the bridge with him this afternoon.

Worse, it had been her own idea.

She reached back to turn the knob, then went for her coat. As she stood in the kitchen doorway pulling on her hat, Thomas leaned over Mama's plants. "This one's growing strong."

"Geranium," Mama said.

Bird pulled on her coat, feeling sadness deep in her chest, remembering the day the baby had been born. She'd never have that again.

Thomas was still talking to Mama. He would have stood there talking to her for a half hour and Mama wouldn't have minded one bit.

Bird took a good look at him. His shoes were scuffed much worse than hers. Had he even combed his hair today? Two buttons were missing from his coat, and he held the whole thing together with one arm crossed over the other.

It didn't take much to use a needle and thread. But then she smiled at herself for being such a know-it-all. Last night she'd tried crocheting a collar, and Annie'd had to rip out the first three rows of the lace because she had made so many mistakes.

She sighed. "Just let me get the button jar. I'll sew on those buttons."

"Never mind," he said, embarrassed, but she made a face. She told herself she was going to die of the heat in her own coat as she rummaged in the jar for two of Hughie's old buttons and sewed them on. Where was his mother? Where was that Lillie, taking herself through Europe with her pearls and her buffed nails while her son was such a mess?

She handed the jacket back to Thomas.

"Thanks, Eldrida," he said as they went down the stairs.

She raised her hand. "Never mind."

Outside, they walked along Water Street toward the bridge. "Does your mother write to you?" she blurted out.

He was running a stick over the wrought-iron railings. The clatter of it was irritating, but everything seemed too quiet when he stopped.

At first he didn't answer. That gave her time to feel sorry for asking.

"She—" He began to run the stick over the railings again. "She's very busy, but—"

They crossed the street to get closer to the bridge, and perched there on the end of a pile of wood. Mounds of debris rose around them, chunks of granite, bent nails as wide as her thumbs, and dusty rocks. They watched the barges going up the river, the froth of their wakes white and cold, and then shaded their eyes to look at the towers, one on the Brooklyn side, the other on the Manhattan side, and in between them men in their small swings, working on the cables that would hold the roadbed up.

A woman in a garnet skirt and black shawl went past, and Bird nudged Thomas. "That's the woman who's finishing the bridge. Her name is Emily, Mrs. Roebling."

Thomas nodded. He pulled his book out of his pocket and began to write. Bird tried to look over his shoulder, but a pale sun was in her eyes. All she could see was that most of the page was filled with his scrawl, and that her name was at the top.

She leaned closer, but he reached out and held her wrist the way Mama had a little while ago. "I'll show it to you someday," he said. "But not now."

Spring 1876

CHAPTER TWENTY-THREE
{BIRD}

For lunch Saturday they'd had boiled potatoes with snips of chives from Thomas's plant, and butter dripping onto the plate. Annie was working a half day at the factory, and Mama had left to take the trolley to visit Aunt Celia. Bird didn't know where Hughie was, but for once she wasn't going to worry about him. She had a whole scoop of time free to read.

But first she stood at the kitchen window angling her head to look at the top of the bridge tower. Even though she couldn't see it very well, she knew that the top was crowded with men—maybe seventy or eighty of them, Da said. *"It's cold up there, Birdie. And the wind! It roars across that great height."*

Mrs. Daley had had something to say about that wind, her arms crossed over her chest. *"Men have been killed that way. A shame and a waste for a bridge that will never work."*

Bird went over to the table. She was halfway through Sister Raymond's book. It was about the terrible famine in Ireland thirty years earlier. It was Mama's famine, she realized, Da's famine. She thought of Da saying, *"Ah, Bird, you'll never really know what it was like. How far we've come."*

The downstairs door opened. Bird put her finger between the pages of the book, listening to the footsteps: too heavy for Thomas's, too light for Annie's, too steady for Mr. Neary's.

The knock came on their door, more a scratch than a knock. Bird pulled it open, startling the girl waiting there. She wasn't much older than Annie, but already there was the beginning of a line between her eyebrows. She had the Viking color of the people from the west of Ireland, and Bird could hear Mama's brogue in her voice. "Are you the healer?"

Bird shook her head. "I'm sorry, she's not here."

"You go with her sometimes, don't you?" the girl said. "I saw you last summer in the street, carrying her bag." She leaned forward. "I know you do."

Bird swallowed. "No, I can't." From the doorway, she could see Thomas on the stairs looking down at them.

"I'll pay you." The line between the girl's eyebrows deepened. "Just what we've always paid your mother. Really, I will." The girl gripped Bird's arm so hard she felt the pain of it. "You have to come."

"No. I can't help." Bird raised her shoulders helplessly, her hands out. "You'll have to get the doctor." But as she said it she could see Thomas on the landing now, shaking his head, reminding her that they had seen the doctor driving his horses hard a few hours ago. He'd never be back in his office yet.

"They will die then." The girl's mouth was chapped, tight and pinched, her skin dry. Mama would say she looked woebegone, but as Bird looked at her eyes, the word she thought of was *desperate*.

"Bird," Thomas said.

For a moment she looked up at him; then she asked, "Who is it that's sick?"

"Just come," the girl said. "My baby sister—"

"But your mother . . . Isn't your mother there?"

"She's sick. Please."

Bird still might not have gone, but she thought of Mary Bridget that summer day, the happiest day she could remember. And Thomas was still standing there, and she knew he wanted her to go. "Wait," she said. "Just—"

She went to the coat stand and leaned her head against the wooden bar. She couldn't do this. She knew she couldn't. But then with her heart pounding hard enough so she felt it in her throat, she reached for her coat, her hat, and pulled open the kitchen drawer for the cure book, spilling out knives and spoons. It wasn't there.

She hurried into her room to search under the bed, and to push back the closet curtain to see if she had left it on the floor. Always missing, that book, but she told herself she knew every line of it by heart. She decided to go without it.

Thomas was at the doorway now. "I'll go with you, and wait outside."

Thomas. Always there.

Downstairs there was a line at the bakery door. Sullivan had fresh bread, and there was a tray of Annie's cookies in the window. Bird threaded her way around the women.

It was an easy walk: three blocks down, one over, and the girl began to talk as they crossed the street. "I don't know what's the matter," she said. "My mother is sick, my sister, my brother."

"Three of them?" Bird's voice didn't sound like her own. "How sick?"

The girl didn't answer.

How was she going to do that, take care of three of them? She cut off the thought as the girl went on. "They have fever. They're burning up, I've covered them, kept them warm, but their faces—" She waved a chapped hand in front of her own face. "And myself—"

Bird took a quick look at her, but she seemed healthy, her cheeks rosy, her eyes clear. *Stay healthy*, she told the girl in her head.

The family lived on the first floor. As they went up the steps in front, Bird caught a glimpse of someone in a bed near the window.

"I'll be right here, Bird," Thomas said, sitting on the stoop and pulling out his writing book.

The apartment inside could have been the Mallons' except there was only one bedroom. The little boy and his mother were in the bed together, the boy's arms flung out, one of them across his mother's body, blotches of red across his face.

A flat rash, red. Scarlet fever. She knew it right away.

She remembered Mama at the kitchen table talking about rashes: chicken pox, smallpox, measles, ringworm.

Scarlet fever.

The mother and the boy didn't seem to know Bird and the girl were there, and even when the girl said, "I've brought help," they didn't open their eyes.

Help. What help could she be?

She stared down at them. Anyone could see how sick they were. "Where is the baby?"

The girl turned. "There."

The tiniest baby lay in the middle of the bed, her hair soft and fine across her head, her eyes closed, her lashes dark on her cheeks, the rash across her face. She was so still.

Bird stepped back from the bed, taking deep breaths, and even in that terrible moment, she remembered seeing Mama doing that once. She had wanted Mama to hurry, almost saying it aloud. *Hurry, Mama, open your bag, do something, Mama.*

Was it possible Mama hadn't known what to do either?

The boy was nearest to her. She put her hand on his forehead, and felt the heat of it. The only thing she remembered from all the times with Mama, from all the lines she had written in the cure book, was: *Feed a cold, starve a fever.* Or was it the other way—*starve a cold, feed a fever?*

Think, she told herself, and remembered having the grippe one winter. Mama had washed her face, her arms, her legs with cold water, water that had made her shiver but had felt so good.

Bring the fever down. Yes.

She pulled the covers off the bed, seeing their thin legs.

"What are you doing?" the girl said. "They'll freeze."

She could see Thomas outside, sitting there. Waiting for her.

In Mama's voice she asked for clean rags and a pan of cold water, and while she waited, she stood next to the bed, her hands clenched, and she didn't dare reach out to the baby.

The girl brought everything, water sloshing onto the floor.

"Go now for the doctor," Bird said. She wanted to do that herself, wanted to rush out of the room and down the street. *Please let the doctor be there*. She wanted to pound at his door and bring him there, and then go home, where she didn't have to think about people with terrible fevers, and a baby that looked as if she wasn't alive, her hands like stars on her small chest. *Please*.

Head down, the girl glared at her.

"Do it now." Bird felt as if she couldn't breathe.

"But the money," the girl said.

Money. What did she care about money?

A sound came from the bed, but she didn't know which one of them had moaned, or sighed, or even mumbled something.

She tore the rag in two and dropped both halves into the water. "You don't have to pay me. Use it for the doctor."

"We have no money. There's no money here in the house," the girl said. "Not a cent."

Bird began with the boy first, his forehead, his cheeks, his neck, and in an instant, the rag was warm from his skin. She dropped it back into the pan and squeezed out the other one. She reached for his arm, pushing back the sleeve to see the rash like the patterns on the map in their classroom.

She looked back over her shoulder. "Go now."

"I wasn't going to give you money." The girl's eyes slid away from Bird's. "We'd bring a chicken to your mother when we could. My father works at the poultry market, and sometimes they give him one or two to take home."

She talked fast, breathlessly, but Bird didn't have time to listen. "I don't care about money and chickens." Her voice was hard. "Get the doctor."

Bird looked back at the boy, and after a few moments she heard the outside door close.

On the far side of the bed, the mother moaned, so she leaned across and dabbed water on her face and neck, then her arms. As she did she thought, *What about the baby?*

She didn't want to touch the baby. Didn't want to know if she was dead. But still she reached down, her arms underneath that small body, and pulled it up against her. The baby was burning with fever.

But alive. Alive!

Bird wiped her with the rag but it wasn't enough. She needed something larger, something to wrap the infant's whole body, but there was nothing in that room. She stood up with the baby in her arms, overturning the pan of water, and went into the kitchen.

With one hand, she reached under the waistband of her skirt and loosened the string of her petticoat. It dropped to her feet and she stepped out of it.

She went to the sink, so grateful that they had running water, and soaked the petticoat, then sank down on the floor to wrap it around and around the baby, to bundle her in that wet cloth. As she did, she felt the baby shudder, saw her face contort, and knew without ever having seen it before that she was convulsing.

Did babies die of convulsions? She didn't know enough, would never know enough.

She put her thumbs into that little mouth, over the small tongue so the baby wouldn't swallow it.

The doctor! The doctor would never come. She would sit there forever, feeling the baby's toothless mouth biting down on her thumbs.

She would never leave that spot, never, never—

But he did come at last, smelling of the outside and of apples from his pipe.

She scrambled up and he took the baby from her, looking down at Bird's face, but she slid away from him and out the door onto the dark street.

And like a shadow, Thomas was there. He took her arm, and they went home together. She heard him saying, "All right, Birdie. All right."

CHAPTER TWENTY-FOUR
{THOMAS}

What had happened in there? What had it been like for Bird? Thomas didn't ask, didn't say a word, but followed her up the stairs.

Mrs. Mallon must have heard them coming, because she was standing in the doorway. "Where have you been, Birdie? Thomas? I've been worried!"

He moved around them and started up to his apartment.

"Don't go, Thomas." Bird shrugged out of her coat, leaving it outside the door, and held her hands out so she didn't touch anything.

Mrs. Mallon's hand went to her mouth. "What is it, child?"

"Do you die of convulsions? Do you die of scarlet fever?"

Thomas remembered having scarlet fever, and the woman with the lace on her sleeves bending over him.

Mrs. Mallon was shaking her head. "What are you talking about, convulsions? Scarlet fever?" She went to the sink and turned on the faucet. "Where have you been?" She looked over her shoulder at Thomas.

"A girl came," he said. "Her family was all sick."

He watched her wash Bird's face gently, rubbing the brown soap over her hands and wrists. Then Bird dried her hands on a towel and sank down opposite him.

"There was a mother. A boy in bed. A baby—" She broke off, then began again, telling her mother all of it.

She could hardly get the words out, Thomas saw that, but her voice was stronger when she looked up at her mother. "I don't know enough, and maybe I didn't do the right thing. They could be dead because of me, all of them."

It seemed that she talked forever. "I don't even know the baby's name. I don't know any of their names."

And all the while, he thought of what he had written in his book about her. He'd always known he'd show it to her someday. What was the use of writing if someone didn't read what you had to say? But he'd pictured saving it until he was sure she'd want to see it.

Mrs. Mallon was running her rough hands over Bird's hair. "Don't you think that happens to all of us?" she said. "Oh, Birdie, there's another part to all this. Sometimes it works."

"But sometimes it doesn't," Bird said, her voice so low he could hardly hear it.

"That's true. But when you can help, the feeling inside is so great, is so wonderful, that it makes the hard times all worthwhile." He could see the flash of tears in Mrs.

Mallon's eyes. "Just think, Bird. How would you feel if you saved them?"

Bird looked down at her hands, shaking her head, then went over it again, what she had done, the covers pulled back, the water, the petticoat.

Mrs. Mallon listened, her head tilted. "Terrible to look at, a convulsion," she said.

Thomas sat there a little longer, then went upstairs quietly to find one of his writing books. He wished his handwriting had been a little better, but still he knew she'd be able to read it.

He took out the picture of Lillie and left it on the table.

Pop was rustling around in the kitchen. "I'll be back soon," Thomas said. "We'll have a little soup or something."

He went downstairs and opened the door without knocking. They were still at the table, teacups in front of them, and he saw there was one poured for him.

He put the book in front of her and waited as she opened it slowly.

He knew what she'd be reading first as she started from the beginning, reading what he'd had to say when he was younger, and then growing older, stories at first about tiny mice who lived in families in back of the wall, and stories about school, and apartments in Greenpoint and Canarsie and Flatbush, elves in Ireland that he'd pictured as Pop had told him about them, and the woman with lace on her sleeves.

She kept turning pages, and then halfway through, she whispered, "Water Street."

Thomas knew she was reading now about a boy who

listened at a register, thinking about a family, and a light-house, and then she turned the next page and took a breath.

It was the story he really wanted her to see: a story about a girl who thought less of herself than everyone else did, who worried about everyone, even when she didn't want to, even when it made her irritable. A girl who was afraid, and who hardly knew it yet, but was on her way to being a healer like her mother, because there'd never be anything else for her, and how lucky they were just to know her.

"Oh, Thomas," she said.

He felt it in his chest, so glad he had let her read it.

Mrs. Mallon looked across at him. "I'm making dinner."

He shook his head. "Tonight I'll eat with Pop."

He took the book from Bird and started for the stairs. She came after him, but before she could say anything, he waved and hurried inside.

CHAPTER TWENTY-FIVE

{BIRD}

They'd stayed up late the night before, much later than usual, Bird reading a piece of Sister Raymond's book to everyone. They'd all overslept in the morning. She and Annie darted around each other getting dressed, no time for oatmeal or bread warmed over the stove.

Mama was out first, and then Annie, who leaned back to tell her, "Just take the newspapers out for me, leave them in the areaway with the ashes."

Bird grabbed her schoolbooks under one arm, the papers in an unruly pile under the other. Two days' worth, the *Standard Union*, the *Brooklyn Daily Eagle*.

She stood on the steps to feel the spring breeze that tossed up dust in the street like tiny cyclones. She went into the areaway and dropped the papers next to the ash cans.

Immediately a wind took the papers, blowing them down

the alley. Halfheartedly she went after them. And as she stooped over, she saw the picture on the front page.

Lillie in her gown and the pearls around her neck.

But not Lillie Neary.

Not Thomas's mother at all, but a famous actress, Lillie Langtry. She'd even heard that name before.

Bird closed her eyes, crumpling the picture in her hand. She couldn't leave it there to blow around, for Thomas to find. She tore it out of the newspaper and folded it into her notebook before she closed the gate and went down the street, hurrying to get to school before the bell chimed.

Thomas was crossing the street behind her. They hadn't had time to call him for breakfast, and he must have had bread and jelly by himself upstairs. Crumbs littered his shirt, and a tiny spot of jelly dotted his collar. No Lillie. No mother to clean him up. Dear Thomas, poor Thomas.

She'd remembered sugar for the horses, and she stopped to feed one quickly, her hand flat, feeling the softness of the horse's mouth. Thomas held out sugar for another one, and two girls from their class passed on the other side of the street, smirking because Thomas and Bird were there together.

The day passed, and she forgot how tired she was. They solved science problems and arithmetic examples. In back of her, Mary Dwyer gave her two cherry lozenges, and she left one next to the inkwell for Thomas.

When the day was almost over, Sister Raymond reminded them how important good penmanship was. In her large, even handwriting she wrote an exercise on the blackboard for them to copy.

Bird dipped her pen into her inkwell and opened her notebook. Staring up at her was the picture, the famous English actress with her name splashed across the bottom: *Lillie Langtry.*

Before she could grab the paper, it fluttered off her desk and lay on the floor between her and Thomas. She reached down quickly, but his hand was there first. He scooped up the paper and put it in his pocket.

The minutes dragged. Bird wrote the exercise in her book, the letters shaky, until Sister Raymond stood up from her desk. "Time to go home."

Thomas didn't look at her. He walked out the door without stopping for his jacket.

She put on her own coat feeling sick to her stomach, folded Thomas's coat over her arm, and hurried home.

Upstairs the door was closed, and she left his coat on the newel post. Instead of going inside she sank down on the step. Should she go up there? What could she say to make things better?

She wanted to put her head down on her knees and close her eyes. She felt the way she had years ago when she'd tumbled down the stairs and had the wind knocked out of her: a pain in her chest and stomach so strong it was hard to breathe.

She thought of him walking home with her after the scarlet fever family. *"All right, Birdie. All right."* And the story he had written in his book about her becoming a healer. A wonderful story, even though it wouldn't happen. It gave her a feeling of such warmth to know how he felt about her. She remembered cold nights walking to the yard together to bring Da his dinner, and the book. Oh, the book.

She turned her head thinking she might cry, but it was too much for tears.

She heard the front door open, and Mr. Neary's footsteps. He was singing loudly as he came up with slow stumbling steps.

And then she did cry, great gulps of tears.

He stopped. "What's the matter, girlie?" He fished for her name. "Eldrida, is it?"

"I've done a terrible thing to Thomas."

"Don't worry about Thomas," he said. "Thomas is all right."

How could he say that? Without thinking, she stood, blocking his way upstairs. "Thomas is not all right." She was two steps above him, almost face to face. "And you," she said. "You've done worse than I."

His face changed, and she saw him put his hand up to his mouth.

"You're a terrible father," she said, and realized she was shouting, even as she wondered how she dared say what she was saying. But it was true, she told herself. True.

She leaned closer to him. "There's no one finer in the whole world than Thomas Neary."

"Do you think I don't know that?" he said.

She heard something and turned. The door to the apartment upstairs was open, and Thomas was standing there. "I'm sorry, Thomas," she said. "I'm so sorry."

Mr. Neary scuttled past and went up the last flight as

Thomas came down slowly. She saw how tall he was now, a head over her, his face bonier. She saw how he would look in a few years when he was grown. "I'm all right, Bird," he said as they sat down on the bottom step. "It's just what I wanted to believe."

"Oh, Thomas, I know. If only I hadn't put the newspapers out," she said. "If only I hadn't seen the picture."

He grinned at her. "No one finer in the world," he said.

She ducked her head, not knowing what to say. But then she smiled up at him.

CHAPTER TWENTY-SIX
{THOMAS}

Pop sat at the table in the living room, a bowl of soup in front of him. His hands were too shaky to lift the spoon, so Thomas held up the bowl to sip.

"So what was all that about, Thomasy? Did you have a fight with that lovely girl?" He stopped for another sip. "I think she was angry at me."

"It was about my mother," Thomas said.

"The soup tastes fine, Thomasy. There's nothing like it when you're under the weather."

Thomas put the bowl down. "I want to know," he said.

"About the soup?"

He reached out, grabbing Pop's wrist. "I'm almost a man," he said. "No matter what it is. No matter how terrible she was."

Pop reached for the soup bowl, raising it to his lips, a few drops spattering on his waistcoat. "What are you thinking then? What do you mean, terrible?"

Pop's eyes were bleary, Thomas thought, but he wasn't so bad that he didn't know exactly what was going on. "I'll leave you if you don't tell me. I'll walk out this door and down the stairs, and I'll never come back." He could hear the thickness in his throat and in his words. He had no money, and the thought of never seeing Bird again was impossible, but he said it again, and knew he meant it. "I need to know. I will leave unless you tell me."

The cup clattered on the table. "You will be sorry to know, Thomasy."

Was that true? And then he thought that knowing would be better than thinking about it every day, not sure if she had left him because she didn't care about him.

"You were not the first." Pop ran his hands across the dusty table, leaving clean lines.

"What do you mean?"

"You had a brother, just a year old. A boy with soft dark hair." He sighed. "And you an infant." Pop's lips were trembling. "But there was fever in the sixties, and the boy died, wasting away, and she blamed herself. She was sick, I think, and she left thinking you'd be sick next, and it would be her fault. So she took herself away. She couldn't bear seeing you with a fever like that, seeing you die."

Thomas looked up. "She could be alive then. She could be somewhere."

Pop shook his head. "She is not alive." His hand went to

his mouth. "I couldn't even look for her. I had you to take care of."

Thomas felt as if he could hardly breathe. He waited.

"They found her in the water at the base of the Hudson Pier. She had drowned."

"Killed herself?" Thomas asked, his voice not sounding like his own.

"We don't know that. She had fever." Pop was quiet. "I never guessed you thought she was terrible. I thought maybe you didn't think of her at all."

He leaned forward, touching Thomas's wrist, and Thomas could feel the tremor in it. "She loved you, Thomasy."

Thomas stood up facing Pop, feeling something in his chest so big, so huge, loving him. "What was her name?" he asked.

"Maura."

Maura.

And when he could talk: "I would like to know what she looked like."

Thomas could see Pop trying to put it into words. "You could walk down the streets of Brooklyn and look at any Irish woman. Freckles and dark hair. Small features."

"There was another woman," Thomas said.

Pop shook his head. "Ah, you remember. It was her sister, Nellie. She came to help us, but went back home to Granard after a while."

He stood up. "I'm in need of something to warm my bones this night."

"This is why you drink? All this time—"

Pop shook his head. "I always drank. Even when I was your age. It's hard to know why."

Thomas didn't try to stop him. He went back into his room and sat on the bed.

He had found out what he needed to know at last, and somehow he had a family now. A brother who had died young, and sometime he'd ask Pop his name. And a mother, Maura.

One day he might even say to someone, *"I had an aunt who taught me that writing would be everything for me."*

The apartment didn't seem so empty now,.and from the register he could hear someone talking. He thought he'd go downstairs after all. He knew they'd be glad to have him stay for dinner.

CHAPTER TWENTY-SEVEN
{BIRD}

It was Saturday again, later in April, one of Da's rare days off, and he and Mama had gone to see Aunt Celia.

"You'll be all right for supper, Bird?" Mama had asked on her way out the door. "There's cheese and leftover meat, and Annie will be home soon."

Bird waved them down the stairs, then curled up in the big kitchen chair to read, until she heard the outside door open, and footsteps coming up the stairs. Too early for Annie.

She put her book down and went to the door.

Standing before her was the girl with the blond hair and the line between her eyes. In her hand she held a chicken, pale and plucked.

"Come in," Bird said.

The girl shook her head. "I am beholden to you," she said. "And this poor chicken is nothing for what I owe you."

The girl reached out and took Bird's hand to wrap her fingers over the chicken's scaly yellow legs. "I won't forget."

Bird stood there, not moving, not able to speak as the girl started down the stairs again. Then she took a step forward and leaned over the banister. "Alive? Are they alive?"

The girl smiled up at her. "Would I have brought you a chicken if they weren't?"

She went down the stairs, and Bird went back into the kitchen to put the chicken on the ice. She sat at the table, remembering what Mama had said: *How would you feel if you saved them?*

The feeling was indescribable. She couldn't read; she could barely think. By the time she heard Annie's footsteps on the stairs it was almost dark.

Annie sank down in the chair opposite Bird, leaning over to unbutton her shoes. "Thomas is outside," she said. "He's looking for you."

"Always there, that Thomas," Bird said.

"Take pity on him, Bird," Annie said, grinning. "I'm going to sleep. Sleep for an hour, sleep for two . . ." Her voice trailed off.

Bird went downstairs to see Thomas leaning against the gate in front of the house, his cap pulled down over his eyes.

"You don't have to wait for me every two minutes, Thomas Neary," she said.

"I was going to come up for you if Annie hadn't sent you down," he said. "I didn't want to tell her, but I saw Hughie take the ferry across to Manhattan. I know there's a fight in New York tonight. I heard it on the street this morning."

She had a sudden picture of Hughie fighting, sweat-covered, knuckles bleeding.

"It's in the back of a saloon in New York, a place called McCormick's."

She stood looking up Water Street. People hurried along as the sky darkened. What should she do? Then they started for the ferry, knowing they were going after Hughie without either of them having to say it.

"What about your ma?" Thomas asked.

"She and Da are with Aunt Celia, and Annie's napping. She'll be asleep for hours unless someone wakes her. We're all right."

They went as quickly as they could toward the new Fulton Ferry building at the end of the street. The boat was still in the slip, almost filled with passengers. Breathless, they edged through the gate just before the guard clanged it shut.

"I have money," Thomas said. "Just enough."

"Sorry," she said. "I never thought—" And then the ferry rumbled beneath them, crashing into the pilings with a wrenching sound as it moved onto the river. She hated that sound, remembering the man who had designed the bridge, John Roebling, whose foot had been crushed against those pilings.

The boat lumbered along, the water churning in back of them, digging up a pale wake, as the broad prow of the boat tossed aside filthy bits of litter. She began to shiver, but not because she was cold.

They leaned against the railing, wedged in between two men eating thick meat sandwiches. One man pointed out the huge Brooklyn tower that they were leaving behind, and then the top of the New York tower as it came closer. "Finished by June."

"Maybe," the other said, waggling his huge hand back and forth. "Maybe not."

Bird glanced down at her own hands. *Square hands, smooth hands,* Thomas had written about her. Hughie's hands were large, and square, but so much stronger. Years ago he used to lift her to the window to see the ferry, or snow falling on Water Street, or a storm with lightning flashing across the sky. Years ago clapping her hands in his.

Hands that would be cut tonight from boxing.

When she found him, she'd beg him not to do it. She'd hold on to his hand and wouldn't let go until she brought him home. She promised herself that. She would make him listen.

The ferry groaned into the landing on the New York side of the river and hit the pilings with a screech. Last ones on, they were first off, and they stood in the street to get their bearings.

How different Manhattan was from Brooklyn: the buildings higher, the streets dirtier. On their side it was almost like the country, but here it was really a city. Men lay on the corners; a bottle was flung out of a window, just missing them; horses and wagons filled the streets.

Thomas pointed the way, and Bird followed, threading her way around people, crossing the street, her sleeve up to her nose when she saw a horse carcass lying in front of them, gray and bloated.

The sign up ahead said MCCORMICK'S FINE ALES. One of

the letters was missing in FINE, so it read FIN. A poor-looking place. People were milling around outside. She tried to push past them to get in, but she was shoved back. There were so many: a man in filthy work clothes standing next to someone in a top hat and tails, women with their lips rouged, their dresses with metallic beads that glinted in the light spilling out from inside.

She couldn't see much through the window. A mist of steam from the heat inside covered the glass, and water ran in rivulets as if it were raining.

She listened to the shouts. Voices rose and fell as the boxing matches went one way and then another. "They're killing him," someone said, and she remembered Officer Regan saying one time: "*A punch from a fist will kill someone, and they'll lock him up for homicide.*"

She grabbed Thomas's hand and pushed hard on the back of the person in front of her. She stepped on feet, used her elbows, and people parted around her. She pulled Thomas after her as they squeezed through the door.

One of Hughie's friends was standing just inside, one of that gang, Sons of Sligo. Her family hadn't come from County Sligo, they had nothing to do with Sligo. She could feel rage hard in her throat. She grabbed his sleeve, knowing she was bruising his skin under his jacket. "Where's my brother?" she yelled above the voices.

"Who—" Then he must have realized who she was. He pulled away from her. "In back. He's been hurt." He raised one shoulder. "The man he fought was too much for him."

A roar came from the circle of people standing in front, and he turned away to see what was happening.

Thomas led the way into a small room with sawdust on the floor, where Hughie lay, surrounded by men. She pushed until she was in front of him. Blood came from his nose, thick and shapeless now, his eyes swollen almost shut, deep gashes in his knuckles, but the worst was a cut over his eyebrow.

A man knelt over him, a bottle of whiskey in his upraised hand, pouring it over the cut.

Her face burned. "Get away from him!" She raised her own hand. The man stepped back and the others fell away, until there was an empty circle around Hughie.

"I have a needle and coarse thread for things like this," someone said.

"Don't touch him."

She saw Hughie angle his head. "I hate what you're doing," she told him, even as she lifted her skirt and tore great strips from the bottom of her petticoat, thinking back to the one she had left wrapped around the baby. She knew how to bandage. She could thank Mama for that.

She wrapped those strips around his hands, and used smaller pieces to pack his nose so the bleeding might stop, and all the time it was circling in her mind: What would she do about the cut over his eye? It was fearful, deep and jagged, but the blood wasn't pulsing, and she was thankful for that.

"Give me the needle," she said to the man.

"I've done this before," he said. "It's going to hurt him."

She looked at the man filthy with the smell of alcohol. "Give it to me."

He handed the needle to her, and she poured the whiskey over Hughie's forehead.

"Do you hear me, Hughie?" she asked. "I'm going to stitch this. I've seen Mama do it, and it couldn't be so different from sewing a coat. . . ." She realized she was babbling and stopped for a moment. "You'll have a scar, but it will be straight and as even as I can do it."

He made a motion with his hand.

She took the needle and tried to push it through his skin. It was harder than she thought, the flesh thicker, but she tried it again, taking the first stitch, knotting the string, and cutting, and then a second one, feeling the anger seeping out of her, a little sick to her stomach, reminded of a roast that Mama would tie together before she put it in the oven.

She lost track of the stitches she took, but then it was finished, and she knew she'd never be afraid to do it again. She looked down at Hughie's ruined face.

They stayed there for a long time, Hughie propped against the wall, and then she and Thomas helped him up. They walked him between them, his arms heavy across their shoulders, and went to the ferry.

Suppose Mama was home? Bird didn't want her to see Hughie. She didn't want any of them to see him. She didn't want to see Mama's tears or hear Da's terrible disappointment.

When they reached the house, she said, "I'll take him down the cellar, but go upstairs yourself. Gallagher's must be closed, and I don't want your father to know."

Thomas hesitated, and then he nodded.

She took the steps down one at a time, slowly, Hughie mumbling something about melting away. How foolish she'd been to be afraid of that cellar. She found mats and an old coat, and helped him lie down; then she leaned against the wall as he slept.

At last he opened his eyes. "Sorry, Bird." His voice was thick, and she saw blood in his mouth. He said something else, and she leaned closer. She thought he'd said, "Wanting what I couldn't have."

"To win?"

He squinted up at her. "To put my hands in the dirt. To farm."

To farm?

Across her mind flashed a picture of the night they'd brought him home from the caisson, crying, writhing in pain. She thought about his holding up two fingers, and the loss of the two dollars a day. Was that it, then? The money for the farm?

She thought of his love for Mama's plants, of his stillness when he listened to the stories of Da's farm in Ireland. How had she not realized?

He slept again.

Later, she saw his eyes on her, slits in his face. She could hardly see their color.

He pulled himself up and ran his tongue over his lips. "I'm all right now," he said, his voice still thick. She thought he was trying to smile, but it was hard to tell. "Not a fighter, either," he said.

"A farmer," she said. "I can see that."

"Ah, Bird," he said, and she leaned forward to hear him. "Da's right. You're like herself."

There was a noise at the top of the stairs, and she heard Mama's footsteps. Mama came toward them, her hand at her throat.

"All right, Mama," Bird said in Thomas's voice. "All right."

Mama looked at Hughie's face, ran her hands over his cheeks. "You did this, Bird?"

Bird gave a quick nod.

Mama raised her head. "Yes, good."

They brought him upstairs, banging back the kitchen door so they could help him in.

Annie came out of the bedroom. "Oh, Hughie," she said. "How could you?"

Bird put up her hand. "It's over now."

And Hughie squinted across at her, nodding.

"Well then," Mama said, "we'll say no more about it."

CHAPTER TWENTY-EIGHT
{THOMAS}

Today was graduation day. He awoke early and lay there listening to the sounds coming from the register. The Mallons were rushing around getting ready for the day, but in his own apartment it was still.

Pop must have forgotten and left already, or maybe hadn't even come home last night.

Yesterday evening, Thomas had been downstairs, Annie pressing his jacket and fussing over the dress Bird had made, telling her, "A pair of sticks wouldn't fit in these openings, much less your arms."

Now he went into the living room, where the sun was streaming through the cracks in the dusty draperies, and he pushed them back to see the two bridge towers, dwarfing everything around them.

He reached up to feel the smoothness of the old velvet. Would it go well today? Everything was ready. Even his speech.

Sister Raymond had picked him for class valedictorian, and afterward he'd told Bird, "A surprise."

She'd looked at him as if he had lost his mind. "Who else? In this whole class there's no one better than you in writing or speaking."

"No one finer," he'd teased her, remembering the day on the stairs.

He thought about his mother, wondering what he would have called her. Bird and Annie called their mother Mama, but Hughie always called her Ma.

And his own mother's sister. He'd called her the woman with the lace sleeves. Had she stayed, he would have had a name for her, too.

He went into the kitchen and put the water on to boil, whispering the speech as he did, for the hundredth time. He pictured himself on the stage, opening his mouth and forgetting all of it.

After the tea, and an egg that he'd boiled, he went in to get dressed. He heard the sound of the door and poked his head out to see Pop coming into the living room. He looked fine standing there, his hands a little shaky, but otherwise steady on his feet.

"It's my graduation day," Thomas said.

Pop nodded. "Don't I know that, Thomasy?"

Pop put on his jacket and patted Thomas's cheek. "The day I found myself alone with you, a squalling baby, I wouldn't have thought it would be possible to get to a day like today. But just look at you. Face clean, shirt clean. You're going to be somebody someday. A man in a top hat."

They both laughed, and Bird called then, "Thomas Neary, are you ever going to be ready?"

And Annie in back of her: "Do you have to raise the roof with your noise, Bird Mallon?"

He went back into the lighthouse bedroom, took his speech from the bed, and looked over the first few lines. He folded it into his pocket just in case, and followed Pop out the door.

CHAPTER TWENTY-NINE
{BIRD}

The smell of pie wafted up from Sullivan's Bakery as they started down the stairs, and outside, Willie, the baker's assistant, waved to them. The sun was shining, and blue skies and wispy clouds were reflected in the windows across the way. The block was busy with women sitting on the steps or standing on the corner talking.

Thomas murmured to himself as he walked next to Bird. Not only was he the valedictorian, but he had also won the prize for the best eighth-grade essay. *How exciting,* Bird thought, *how right,* even though they still didn't know what the prize was.

Bird's own essay was plain: She'd said she didn't know what was going to happen in her life, but she knew it had to have something to do with healing someday. She was satisfied with the essay, and knew Sister Raymond had been pleased with it.

Bird hugged Mama and Da at the auditorium door; then she and Thomas hurried to the classroom one last time. How different everyone looked. How loudly they talked about who was starting work tomorrow, who would start in a week, while Sister Raymond sat at her desk looking serene. Bird felt a lurch in her chest. Of all of them, she thought, she might be the one who'd miss school the most.

They marched into the auditorium and up on the stage just as they had practiced. Sister Raymond said a few words, then nodded to Thomas, and he went to the podium. Bird leaned forward; it was hard not to be nervous for him.

"I'm going to talk about things that seem impossible," he said. "Like the great bridge that has been under construction for as long as we can remember. People said it would never be finished, but all we have to do is look up, and there are the towers in place."

Mrs. Daley should hear this!

Thomas spoke about a mother and father: "So many hardships, and yet they managed to come to this country, as my own father did," he said. "I want them to be proud of me, all three of them." He talked about a brother he'd become close to, and an older sister who cooked for him.

In a seat near the front, Bird could see Annie reach out to touch Mama's arm, her eyes brimming.

Thomas looked across the stage at Bird, then at the audience again. "I wouldn't be standing here telling you this if my best friend, Bird, hadn't shared her family with me."

Bird glanced at Mr. Neary, next to Da, and saw that he was smiling.

"What I want to do is write about them," Thomas said, still looking at Bird. "I think I'll be able to do that. After all, nothing's impossible."

Oh, Thomas, she thought as Ellen Burke went first to receive her diploma, Ellen, who had said, *He gives her candy, they're going to get married.* Her eyes were still wet when Sister Raymond gave her the diploma, and Hughie looked up at her, smiling.

Later that day they had a party. Mrs. Daley came to sit on Hughie's bed and eat a piece of Annie's cake.

"It's boiling hot in here," Bird told Thomas, and they went to sit on the hallway stairs.

"Filthy steps as usual, Eldrida," he said. "I'm going to put this in my book. You'd better hope no one recognizes you."

She sat back grinning at him, thinking of the end of the ceremony. Sister Raymond had announced the prize for the best essay of the class of 1876: a scholarship to the School of the Arts for Thomas Neary.

He'd write his first book there, Bird was sure.

At last the day was over. One by one everyone left, and Bird went back into the kitchen to help Mama and Annie do the dishes.

Everyone was still at the table, and Mama pulled at Bird's sleeve so she'd sit down on the edge of the chair with her. "Already you have more education than Da and I ever did," Mama said. "It gives me great satisfaction."

Bird nodded, remembering Da giving her the book that day, and all the books that Sister Raymond had shared with her.

Da stood up then and went to the cabinet. He opened the little door underneath and took out the farm box.

"You need to go to high school, Birdie."

"Stuff that head with a little knowledge," Hughie said.

She shook her head, not understanding. She glanced across at him. He would never look quite the same as he had before. His nose wasn't as straight and the scar would always be there, but Mama had said Bird had done the best she could. She knew that was true.

"I'd never—" she began.

Hughie interrupted her, looking at the others around the table. "She'll never take the money because she knows how much I want a farm." He smiled. "But there's enough money in my pockets from boxing to get myself to New Jersey. I'll see if Uncle Patch can find me a place to work with him on a farm."

Mama nodded. "Yes, Patch. And there's a huge seed place down in Monmouth. You could work there, I think, if Patch couldn't help."

"But what about you, Mama?" Bird said. "You've always wanted—"

"We do what we have to do," Mama said.

"But the cabbages Da promised you. The roses."

"One day, maybe." She glanced at Da. "But in the meantime, I can do without them."

Annie patted Bird's shoulder. "You might have to use

your own riches, miss," she said. "All those pennies gathering dust on top of the cabinet."

Leave it to Annie. She knew everything.

Bird took it in. She'd go to high school.

Mama might never have her roses or cabbages, but Bird promised herself that someday she'd make Mama proud.

AFTER

Thomas remembered, writing it all down—

That summer of '76, Mr. Mallon had gotten two tickets to watch the first man cross the river; there was one for Bird and one for Thomas.

E. F. Farrington, the master mechanic, blew kisses to the crowd, then climbed onto a wooden seat that dangled from ropes that stretched from one tower to the other.

Thomas reached for Bird's hand as a motor started up, and Farrington sailed across the river.

Boats and factories sounded their whistles, and church bells pealed, and Thomas took courage himself to lean over and kiss Bird for the first time. "It's not every day," he told her, "that we can see the first man ever to cross the great bridge. Just a few more years and the span itself will be finished."

"Ah, poor Mrs. Daley," Bird said. "She'll have to worry about something else now."

That day was just one of the days he'd write about in his book, but there were others:

The day Annie told them she was going to marry Willie, the baker's assistant . . .

The day Hughie bought an acre of land in Belford, New Jersey . . .

The day a method of preventing caisson disease was announced . . .

The day the free library came to Brooklyn . . .

And the day Bird received her diploma from Bellevue Hospital and began to practice nursing.

But what gave him the most satisfaction was going back through the pages to read about his first story appearing in the Saturday Evening Post.

That afternoon he'd bought Bird the largest bag of lemon drops he could find.

"He gives her candy," she had said, remembering too.

PATRICIA REILLY GIFF is the author of many beloved books for children, including the Kids of the Polk Street School books, the Friends and Amigos books, and the Polka Dot Private Eye books. Several of her novels for older readers have been chosen as ALA Notable Children's Books and ALA Best Books for Young Adults. They include *The Gift of the Pirate Queen; All the Way Home; Nory Ryan's Song,* a Society of Children's Book Writers and Illustrators Golden Kite Honor Book for Fiction; and the Newbery Honor Books *Lily's Crossing* and *Pictures of Hollis Woods. Lily's Crossing* was also chosen as a *Boston Globe–Horn Book* Honor Book.

Patricia Reilly Giff lives in Connecticut.